# FROM SHREDS TO RICHES

# FROM SHREDS TO RICHES

## GARRETT WYLAND

WITH

David Fisher

"I was skeptical when a friend gave me this book to read. I can't remember the last time a book captured my attention from start to finish. If you want a side splitting look at the greedy world of high pressure selling, then you'll love this book."

"I loved this book. It was such a departure from what I usually read. I highly recommend this book to everyone who enjoys reading. It enthralls the reader."

# CONTENTS

Chapter One


# BOOM! SMASH! - ENTER THE FBI


Scott Newman started his day in his usual style: Ralph Lauren polo shirt, Dolce and Gabbana jeans, custom John Varvatos classic black Moto leather jacket, Gucci slip ons without socks, and a Platinum Presidential time piece with an Ice Blue Dial reflecting the morning light.

A ruggedly handsome man in his mid forties, his eyes are the color of the aqua blue sea surrounding an exotic Caribbean island like Martinique or the waters of Tahiti or Maui. He is often mistaken for a film actor, a career he ironically declined to pursue despite numerous opportunities. A Priority Overnight envelope and two stacks of 'Benjamins' (one hundred dollar bills) lie in the center of his cherry mahogany desk that was meticulously handcrafted by a local Italian artisanal cabinet maker specializing in seventeenth century design. It had been worth the intense research Scott had invested into finding such a gifted craftsman who entertained very private clients.

Scott's well appointed office in his executive suite on the fortieth floor above Fifth Avenue features a panoramic view of the lush green canopy of trees spread like a soft blanket across Central Park in New York City.

The first thing on his agenda is a call to John Morrison from Fabricon Steel in Boise, Idaho. This company has over two hundred and fifty employees and boasts annual revenues of over two hundred million dollars. Fabricon is already on the books with three hundred and fifty thousand dollars in Paid Up Invoices. John is a 'mooch' (a taker only interested in what's in it for him) and he has already received fifty thousand dollars in gifts and he's only one of Scott's deep ocean of 'whale mooches'. (A 'whale' has already taken large gifts of cash in the past).

Scott leans forward from his full grain leather chair, gathers the crisp 'Benjamins' in his hands and starts counting. "Forty seven and forty eight…let me count the ways I love you, my friend… forty nine and bingo, fifty. There you go, John, fifty beautiful 'Benjamins'." He carefully places the cash in the Priority Overnight envelope and seals it up. Argon Industries was doing well, extremely well. Twenty years of sweat and Scott was at the pinnacle of success in his business.

Few believed he could do it. Even fewer had a view of Central Park. Not bad for a guy who started out in the Bronx sweeping the floor of a local jewelry store for two dollars an hour.

Scott picks up his cell phone and taps John's name on the screen, but it goes straight to voice mail. Scott just smiles. No need to leave a message because a couple seconds later, Scott's familiar Porky Pig ring tone fills the room and John, one of Scott's many 'whale mooches', has instantly returned his call.

"Atta boy, John," exclaims Scott with a shit eating grin. Porky Pig is the unique ring tone on Scott's special phone for 'mooches' only. "John, buddy, good to hear from you. How ya been, bro?"

"Great, what's up my brother?" John asks, knowing full well the answer.

"I just sealed a Priority Overnight envelope stuffed with fifty 'Benjamins'. You want the tracking number?"

"Of course!"

"Grab a pen. You ready? E 818 914 758. Track it after five p.m. today, it'll be at your home address tomorrow."

"I love you Scott, that's why you're the 'Benjamin King'."

"John, again enjoy the five thousand and have a Merry Christmas! I put you down for the exact same order we did a couple months ago. Just give me four purchase order numbers and I'll split the order into four separate invoices. That's seven thousand five hundred per invoice and I'll date the invoices ten days apart so you don't get one large invoice for thirty thousand dollars."

"Perfect Scott, let me give you the purchase order numbers."

"I love you John, thanks for the order. We'll talk in six or seven weeks and work up another order!"

"Great," John says. "I'll be looking forward to your call."

Scott picks up the envelope and tosses it onto the growing pile of Overnight mailing envelopes. He rolls his chair across the floor to the doorway and yells down the hall for Doug to hear his best imitation of the Woody Woodpecker money making victory yell:

HEH  HEH  HEH  HEH  HEH

HEH  HEH  HEH  HEH  HEH

HEH  HEH  HEH  HEH  HEH  HEH  HEH

"Just rocked John Morrison for thirty grand."

He wheels back to his desk and picks up his cell to make his next call.

From outside the window a cloud like shadow slowly creeps across his desk. Scott looks up. A pair of eyes are staring directly at him from a jet black helicopter hovering unnaturally close to the window obscuring the sky.

Large yellow letters dominate the copter's fuselage: FBI.

The victory grin slowly dissolves into confusion on Scott's face.

An ear splitting boom from a battering ram blasts the front door of the office suite into splinters and a dozen FBI agents charge through the opening, peeling off to the left and right, flooding the reception area and the open work spaces.

Shock and disbelief have completely wiped out any trace of Scott's celebration.

Dressed in full combat regalia, the agents are prepared to engage and defeat any well armed and hostile enemy. Some are wearing green body armor with Kevlar helmets and toting AR15's with Glock side arms.

The point guy is ready to toss a flash-bang grenade that is designed to temporarily blind and disorient the potentially dangerous occupants. Within seconds they take possession of every corner of the office, alert and prepared to open fire if there is any resistance.

A few of the employees hit the floor spread eagled, others leap to their feet waving hands of surrender high in the air. Most just remain frozen in their chairs.

Taking center stage is a burly African American female agent who barks, "This is a 'raid'. This is an ongoing FBI investigation into the lightbulb telemarketing industry."

"Scott Newman and Doug Kaufman of Argon Industries."

Like the Statue of Liberty, she was holding high over her head, not the torch of freedom, but a warrant.

"I'm Scott Newman, what's this about?"

Doug is nowhere to be found.

She looks around at her captive audience. "We are not closing down your business. We have a warrant to search the premises and confiscate any and all evidence that we deem pertinent to our investigation including all paper work and computer hard drives."

"May we know your name … Ms. ?" Scott asks politely.

"My name is Agent Gloria Perez. Like I said, we are not here to close your business. You may come by our regional office anytime during business hours and make photo copies of your documents for one dollar a copy."

Agent Perez grips the warrant like she was Moses holding the Ten Commandments. According to the FBI, the warrant was equal to God's Law, if not more sacred.

"Mr. Newman, is Mr. Kaufman here?"

Scott looks in the direction of Doug's desk. That's a good question.

Mr. Kaufman was in fact here, but had managed to shrink into his chair until he was barely visible. He would have preferred under his desk.

Doug resembled a broken down veteran of some foreign war except for the inconvenient fact that he was never a soldier. His lack of self-confidence was quite evident if you engaged him in person, however, his uncanny phone skills charmed even the toughest customers into a sale. His telephone voice was his gift; smooth, calming, he quickly became your best friend, priest and confidante within a few short minutes of falling under his spell.

But not today.

Agent Perez sighs in disbelief. "Mr. Kaufman, may we have a word?"

Doug mumbles something and tries to find his feet, then finally struggles to a standing position.

Scott says with encouragement, "Come on Doug, get over here man, we haven't done anything wrong. Let's find out what this is all about."

Doug trudges over like a condemned man shuffling his feet through his final steps to the electric chair.

"Doug, relax buddy, this is some kind of mistake. We'll sort it out. Let's hear what the agent has to say."

Doug finds a spot next to Scott, leans toward him and mumbles, "I know why they're here. They came for my money. We're going to jail."

Scott quietly responds. "Stop waving the white flag Doug, we're not going to jail."

"Agent Perez, would you mind explaining to my partner that this is not an arrest or a conviction, that we are not going to jail."

"Like I said, we are not closing down your business. You're free to continue doing business during the investigation.

In the meantime, send all your employees home because we're going to be here all day. They may return tomorrow."

Scott can't believe this. "You're going to be here all day?"

"That's right, Mr. Newman, all day. Maybe more depending on your level of cooperation."

Scott looks around at the armed agents who stare at him impassively. "Okay. Do what you need to do."

"All right everyone." Scott can see their fear and uncertainty. "Let's wrap things up. Don't worry because we haven't done anything wrong. I have no idea why they are here. This is just a ridiculous misunderstanding that I intend to take care of so just think of this as an extra day off. Go have some fun. See you tomorrow."

Scott shakes his head at the unfairness of the situation. He watches his frightened and shaken employees gather their belongings and gingerly walk past the well armed FBI agents and through the gaping hole in the wall where once there was a door.

Scott addresses Doug so all the agents can hear him. "Hey Doug, why don't we give our wives a call to spare them the indignity and embarrassment of this 'raid'?"

Scott taps Amy's name on his cell phone. "Hi honey, it's me. No, no you're not late for work. We had some uninvited guests show up from the government and the office will be closed for the day so call Doug's wife and go have a long lunch or something and I'll explain when I get home. No, no, no, it's nothing serious. I got it under control. Just a mistake that's all. Don't worry babe, I'll see you later."

Some of the agents are already attacking the file cabinets with gusto and emptying the files and paperwork into sturdy cardboard boxes to be hand trucked away.

Even though Scott's insides are burning with anger, he calmly addresses Agent Perez. "This is a raid? Is this how the government operates? How do you justify a fucking 'raid' by busting down doors of a legitimate business and terrorizing innocent people for a so called 'investigation' into the lightbulb industry?"

"Mr. Newman, we need to communicate without the use of profanity if you don't mind."

"Listen, Agent Perez, if you were me at this moment, I wonder what kind of language you'd be using."

She ignores Scott's comment and turns away.

Scott does not back off. "What is it about the lightbulb industry that calls for this over the top, Hollywood style 'raid'? What is the term you guys use for this 'no knock' invasion? 'Dynamic entry'? Wow, what a great movie title, *Dynamic Entry,* coming to a theater near you. Is this a government tactic trying to get the FBI nominated for some kind of special Oscar for saving America from the dreaded lightbulb industry?"

"Mr. Newman, this warrant makes it a very serious investigation that must be followed through. Everyone here is just doing their job."

"And this 'raid' is part of the job? Maybe you should consider a new job that doesn't require strong armed tactics and the destruction of private property."

"We don't take unnecessary risks. We can't predict what will happen once we enter the premises," retorts Perez.

"How about coming to my office as a civilian a few days before hand to determine the potential dangers, you know, check out the enemy terrain before attacking," I suggested.

"Like I said, we can't predict what might happen."

"So you're saying that the government has the unlimited power to invade a business or a home without warning or due process, destroy property, intimidate, injure and scare the hell out of innocent people and simply excuse it as collateral damage?"

"Mr. Newman, since we're going to be here all day, why don't we just cut the chit chat and the bad attitude."

"Well good luck Agent Perez, you never know who might be hiding in here. Maybe Pablo Escobar or John Gotti. How about Al Capone? Everyone knows they started their lives of crime in the evil lightbulb telemarketing industry."

Her shoulder mounted receiver squawks and she fails in her attempt to suppress a slight smile as she responds to the call.

"No problems. Mr. Newman is cooperating. We should be out of here in a few hours."

Agent Perez turns to Scott and says, "Thank you for your cooperation, Mr. Newman, we appreciate it."

Scott chuckles and shakes his head in disbelief. "I guess you're welcome since all my rights have been suspended."

Scott moves out of the way as a hand truck loaded with boxes from Doug's office wheels past. Doug is fidgeting with his cell phone and glancing at the agents methodically placing his files in boxes.

"Hey Doug, did you call your wife?"

"Yeah, I told her not to come in because we were being raided by the FBI," Doug said defensively.

"Jesus Christ, Doug. Why put the fear of God in her? Can't it wait until we all get home? Maybe break the news with the four of us together after this 'raid' is over. Why spread the panic?"

"Well I'm worried about my money. You know they can take everything don't you?"

"No they can't take everything, Doug. Not unless you're dumb enough to give it to them."

"Nah Scott, that's why they're here."

"You're just a little paranoid man. Relax. They're not after your money. Don't take this so personally. Maybe Buddy was right when he warned me last week that the FBI was snooping around. This might be an industry wide investigation with several other companies going through this same 'raid' bullshit."

"I don't care about those other companies. I care about me. I don't want to lose everything I worked for. That money is thirty years of my life."

"Doug, buddy, forget about your damn money for a second and take a look around you. We built this business together and no matter what happens with this investigation, we're going to fight them every step of the way. Suck it up, man. We're still in business so let's concentrate on that."

"Look Scott, you're always the optimist, but realistically can't you see the government just screwed us. This is probably a trap and every sale we make from now on will be used later as evidence against us. There's no more Argon, Scott, we're done."

"Okay Doug. Whatever you say. Go on home and I'll catch up with you later," Scott sadly agrees.

Okay Doug. Whatever you say. If you only knew that two years ago, Buddy and I formed three independent companies just for a chicken shit occasion like this when I figured you'd quit on me.

Doug sighs again in defeat, "Sorry, man, I don't want to look at this disaster anymore."

"Yeah, I understand Doug. Go on, get out of here. I'll stay here until they leave."

Doug looks forlornly at the door splinters of confetti spread all over the carpet and with his head down, plods out of the office suite.

"Hey Doug, don't let the door hit you in the ass on the way out."

Scott looks directly at Agent Perez. "Oh wait, there is no door."

Scott returns to the reception area and surveys the scene.

Agent Perez follows him and clears her throat. "Mr. Newman, may I ask you a question, off the record of course? I'm just curious why you haven't flooded this place with lawyers yet."

"Listen, Agent Perez, I don't know about you, but most of the lawyers I know are scumbags who would show up just to watch you haul this shit out of here so later on, they could charge me four hundred dollars an hour to put it all back. So tell me, what do you really expect to find here? This is just routine paperwork."

"We wouldn't be here, Mr. Newman, if this was just routine paperwork."

# Chapter Two

## FROM DIAMONDS TO PEARLS

It seems like I've always had a problem with authority figures. I'm talking about the type of person who has more power than you and is basically just a bully or an asshole. Or someone who poses as an authority like an arrogant or pushy salesperson who figures you don't know anything about the product but you'll buy it anyway.

When I was ten years old, my father took me shopping for a special gift for my mother's fortieth birthday. He had mentioned earlier in the week that the birthstone for the month of April was a diamond. I was determined to learn everything I could about diamonds before we bought one.

There were several jewelry stores in the Bronx where we lived and the first one we visited, my father explained to the salesman that he was looking for the finest diamond earrings for his wife's birthday. The salesman didn't greet us or mention his name much less ask about my father's. He just placed several earring samples on the glass counter for my father's inspection.

My father admitted he didn't know much about diamonds or jewelry and figured the salesman should be an 'authority' or at least possess some reliable knowledge and that his advice would be very much appreciated.

I asked the guy his name, but he ignored me and addressed my father. His name was Jim. The diamond earrings Jim recommended certainly looked attractive. They gleamed with a nice light yellow color. He said they were a little more expensive, but after all, it was a special occasion.

"Excuse me sir," I interjected, "but aren't the best quality diamonds supposed to be colorless?" Jim laughed and said that was probably something I just read in a comic book.

I turned to my father and said, "Dad, I researched diamonds all week long and that's what the big diamond companies like Tiffany explained in their brochures - colorless diamonds are the best quality."

My dad stared at Jim and asked him if what I said was true.

Jim dismissed me as a precocious and insolent child. "No offense sir, but he's just a kid."

My father backed up a couple of steps and replied. "And no offense to you sir, but you just lost a big sale because of this kid."

As we left the store, my dad laughed. He said now that we were prepared with valuable knowledge, he was looking forward to hearing the sales pitch at the next jewelry shop.

Sid was brushing crumbs off his tent sized shirt and closing up the extra large donut box when he noticed us enter his shop. My dad made the same request and Sid explained that he was the store manager and called over a young saleswoman, Nancy, who asked a few questions and then displayed a beautiful pair of colorless diamond earrings.

She got right to the point. "Colorless are top quality sir, you don't want to settle for anything less. Diamonds are usually an expression of love like engagement rings, but your choice for her fortieth birthday is a gift that demonstrates your love for her is forever."

"Can I ask you a question, Nancy?" I just wanted her to pay attention to me for a minute. "Did you know that the word 'diamond' comes from the Greek language and it means 'invincible'?"

She looked at me in amazement and asked how old I was.

When I said ten, she was very surprised and then thanked me for sharing that remarkable fact. Charming a lady at my age was not my intention, but it certainly was the result.

Sid had been observing the whole scene and told me to come back in a few years and he'd give me a job. I told him I was ready to start right now.

The three adults all enjoyed a nice laugh. I did not back down. "I'm serious. I want to start now. It sure looks to me like you could use someone to sweep the floor and polish the glass cases."

"That's true," Sid admitted, "but you're only ten years old and you should be in school all day."

"I'll come by after school every day and work for just one hour and go right home."

Sid shrugged and asked my dad what he thought about it.

"The word 'no' does not mean a thing to my son. Once he sets his mind to something, you can't stop him."

Working for an asshole like Sid was always a challenge for an adult much less a ten year old kid. I learned quickly to ignore his motor mouth that spewed nothing but negative garbage. Most people couldn't take it and Sid would have to hire a new salesperson every week or two. But as for me, his bullshit was nothing more than water off a duck's back. Praise or compliments from him was never going to happen. He paid me on time and that's all I really cared about.

A couple of years went by and Sid was now managing two of the six stores in the Golden Jewelers chain. Although he never admitted it, he was very pleased with my work. He asked me if I had time to clean a second store and I said sure, as long as you double my pay for double the work. He knew it was a waste of breath to argue with me.

By the time I was eighteen and graduated from high school, I had worked my way up the food chain as a stock boy, delivery guy and sales assistant. Instead of attending college, I became a full time salesperson in one of Sid's stores making two hundred and fifty dollars a week with no commissions.

My high school buddy Rob needed a job and Sid hired him as a sales assistant. "The best part about working in a jewelry store," I told him, "is the clientele, mostly females and believe me, some of them are outrageously hot. But when they come through the door, they become kids in a candy store. Our job is to help them pick out the candy. And once in a while, someone will be more than happy to express their appreciation by inviting you out for a 'coffee' or something after the sale. That ain't gonna happen at Walmart."

On the other hand, I gave him a 'heads up' about the worst part of working in that jewelry store - Sid the Sleaze, who was now the general manager of all six Golden Jeweler stores. Even though we didn't see him every day, I warned Rob that the slime ball liked to show up whenever he felt like it and give everyone a rash of shit just because in his small mind he was the big bad boss.

If you were a customer, you'd think the weasel was here to rob the place or maybe just looking for directions to the nearest Golden Corral Buffet. I'd been working for the guy for eight years and he rarely changed his clothes more than once a week or considered taking a shower. Breath mints were out of the question.

Every time he came by, he would throw a roll of paper towels in my direction and bark out like a wannabe Marine Corp drill sergeant to shine the display cases so he could see his reflection on the glass. Rob and I laughed because no one really wanted to see his face or his reflection.

Rob was still a bit uneasy about working for a jerk like Sid, but I reminded him that I had been with Sid for eight years and the trick for dealing with him was simple. Ignore the bullshit and keep your eye on the prize: the consistent weekly pay checks.

Matt was a high school acquaintance of mine who worked as a sales rep for Lumina Pearls, a company based in Beverly Hills, California. He had been coming into the store almost every day for over a week trying to recruit Rob and me for this pyramid scheme. If he could bring us aboard, Matt would receive an override not only on our sales, but on the sales of everyone we would bring into the business.

"Come on guys, think about it," he declared with great confidence. "I'm making more in less than two hours in a single evening than you are in a whole week and all my customers are ladies primed to buy jewelry."

"Okay Matt, tell me how this works?" I asked seriously.

Matt continued without skipping a beat. "We conduct what we call 'Treasure Hunts' in the home of a female customer who functions as the hostess. She invites her friends, relatives, acquaintances and whoever else she can think of to come over and enjoy a pearl diving experience. Hopefully, at least ten or more women show up, giving the hostess an opportunity to earn up to one hundred and fifty dollars in free fourteen karat gold jewelry.

I have a tub of water filled with genuine oysters imported from the oyster beds of Japan. The ladies take turns plucking an oyster from the tub for which they have paid a nominal cost of five dollars per oyster. Every oyster is guaranteed to reveal a cultured pearl and the anticipation builds like a forest fire because sometimes two or three pearls may pop out in a variety of shapes and colors. I'm sure you can imagine the joyful pandemonium that follows such a discovery.

Now that the ladies have been properly primed, refreshments are served for the group while I meet with each lady, one at a time, in a separate room and present a tempting array of fourteen karat gold jewelry available for purchase as a setting for their pearls. During any given evening, I usually sell an average of five hundred to one thousand dollars' worth of jewelry with a healthy commission of forty per cent."

Without hesitation I asked, "When's your next 'Treasure Hunt'?"

Matt smiled and handed me a piece of paper. "Seven o'clock tonight. Here's the address. You're going to be amazed."

I don't know where it came from, but a huge wave of natural confidence swept over me. Holy shit, I can do this!

"Hold on a second Matt. How about letting me run the 'Treasure Hunt'. I know pearls and gold jewelry like the back of my hand and I have no doubt I can hit a home run."

"You know what, that's a great idea, Scott. You already have the natural charm and charisma to wow the ladies, and besides, I'm sure the experience will easily convince you to sign up with Lumina Pearls."

Rob and I arrived together in a lower class neighborhood consisting of modest homes in need of paint jobs and a bit of landscaping. Older model cars filled the street. I looked around shaking my head with doubt. "Rob, can you believe it's possible to sell five hundred to a thousand dollars' worth of jewelry to these housewives in a poor neighborhood like this? We'd be lucky if we sold fifty dollars worth of jewelry to the entire group tonight. This I gotta see."

We were greeted warmly by the hostess as we entered her home, but there were only three other ladies in the living room. I tried not to show my disappointment. In a low voice I asked Matt how the hell could we sell Tupperware much less jewelry. This was going to be a complete waste of time.

"Relax Scott, not a problem. This isn't the first time there's been so few women in attendance. You never know what's going to happen. Just work your sales magic and enjoy the show."

Matt introduced me to the ladies as his partner and mentioned that I would be conducting the 'Treasure Hunt' that evening. I deleted the lingering doubts in my mind and shifted confidently into positive work mode.

I stood next to the Lumina Pearls flip chart mounted on a sturdy wooden easel, beamed my warmest smile, and welcomed the ladies to the 'Treasure Hunt'. "This evening will be a great adventure. It's called a 'Treasure Hunt' because you will be searching for genuine cultured pearls and any pearl that you find is yours to keep."

I flipped over the first page of the chart and began.

"What makes a pearl beautiful and valuable? There are several key factors that determine the quality of a pearl including size and color."

Continuing with great enthusiasm, I pointed out that cultured pearls came in a variety of colors, from white to black and every shade in between.

"Size is what determines the value of the pearl when all the other factors are equal. As you know ladies, size matters; the bigger, the better." The ladies laughed and I emphasized, "the best quality pearls in the world come from Japan where oysters are cultivated over a period of three to four years. And that's what we have right here in this room just for you ladies, Japanese Akoya cultured pearls."

The ladies exchanged happy smiles and clapped their hands in anticipation.

I flipped over another page.

"Pearls and gold make a perfect match." The ladies gazed at the dazzling photo of a yellow gold ring setting.

The women were on the edge of their seats in anticipation of the upcoming pearl dive. "So ladies, let's do what we came here to do…search for hidden treasure - and yes, you guessed correctly," pointing to the tub, "your pearls are beautiful, cultured, saltwater, gem quality pearls - the very best."

The women roared with excitement and although there were only three of them, their cries of anticipation permeated the room.

"Let's move on over to the oyster tub," I said as I handed the tongs to Diane, the hostess.

A key part of the 'Treasure Hunt' strategy is arranging beforehand that the hostess goes first so the enthusiasm is not only maintained but intentionally increased. Asking for a volunteer usually results in a delay while the ladies stand around and look at each other wondering who will go first. This energy sapping situation is easily avoided when the hostess has already been given a complimentary oyster for opening her home for the 'Treasure Hunt'.

The ladies gathered around with unbridled anticipation while Diane took the tongs from me and fished around the tub hoping that the oyster she plucked would yield a brilliant pearl.

Everyone was nervously clapping their hands and standing on tip toes as I placed the oyster on a cutting board and carefully opened it with a knife. Tension rose while I took my sweet time. Finally, the oyster yawned wide open and out popped two incredibly beautiful pearls. One was a perfectly white Akoya and the other was champagne colored with a radiant luster.

The ladies gasped in unison and then shrieks of amazement spread through the room and once the initial shock wore off, the ladies jostled for the tongs. I was one step ahead and handed the tongs to the next lucky pearl hunter, a very attractive blonde in her early thirties with legs from here to next week. She was dressed in a tight black mini skirt with killer stilettos that further extended her fabulous legs. I stepped back and nudged Rob. This show was gonna be good.

The blonde bent over the tub from her waist and unintentionally (or not) presented her perfect derriere for our viewing pleasure. I mumbled to Rob how I'd love to pop open that oyster.

She took her time searching for the perfect oyster fully aware of the male audience enjoying the show. She finally made a selection, provocatively stood up in slow motion to prolong the moment and proudly presented the oyster to me.

Holding the knife, I reprised the ceremonial opening of the oyster and the ladies went crazy when a perfect shimmering silver pearl emerged. The pandemonium continued in full force as the remaining two ladies fished their oysters out of the tub and more incredible pearls were revealed. The orgy of pearl selection did not cease until every last oyster was opened. Four ladies emptied out the oyster tub, opening all twenty five oysters. I looked at Rob and winked as I marveled at the unbelievable scene.

Refreshments were served and I looked through the information cards that had been filled out earlier by each attendee with their personal data as well as a check box indicating their interest in hosting a future 'Treasure Hunt'.

In a separate room, a table featuring trays of white gold and yellow jewelry: rings, broaches, necklaces and earrings were presented on a table cloth of richly embroidered pure white Brazilian silk from the exclusive Vale de Sada.

The ladies were called individually for a consultation and hopefully a jewelry sale. I called the name of the first lady and invited her to view the jewelry. Her pearls were displayed on a velvet cloth in front of her and I began. "These are gorgeous pearls, Mary. We always ask our ladies their opinion on our different rings to get an idea of which ones are the most popular because we change our styles every so often. Your opinions are very important to us."

Mary answered a bit reluctantly. "Okay Scott, I think I can help." I set her information card down in front of me and picked up a pen to check off the boxes indicating her answers.

"Just remember I'm not really interested in buying a ring," said Mary somewhat defensively.

"Relax Mary. This is just a survey and we really value your opinions. Are you okay with that?"

"Okay sure, I just wanted to be clear about it," maintaining her defensive posture.

"Great, we appreciate your time. Now tell me Mary, do you prefer white gold or yellow gold?"

"Well actually I adore yellow gold," Mary said cautiously.

I placed the tray of yellow gold rings in front of her. "Go ahead and choose four of your favorites." I removed the larger tray and placed her four selections on a smaller tray.

"Take your time, Mary. Out of these four rings, which two do you like the best?"

Mary pointed to two rings and I removed the other two rings.

"Okay Mary, which one is your favorite?"

"Oh my I love them both. This is not easy," she pondered with a warmer voice.

"Take your time, Mary," I said softly.

"Okay this one," she sighed in relief.

I set the second ring off to the side so her selection now rested in front of her and of course, she couldn't take her eyes from it.

I continued. "Mary, if you were going to wear this ring, would you wear it on your left hand or your right hand?"

She offered her right hand which I took and gently squeezed her fingers. "Would you wear it on your ring finger or pinky finger?"

"My ring finger of course," Mary exclaimed with certainty.

"Do you remember your ring size?"

"I believe it's six and a half."

"Let me make a quick measurement just to be sure," I said confirming her ring size.

Still holding her hand, I took the ring from the tray and slid it neatly onto her finger. I delicately raised Mary's pearl from the velvet cloth and suspended it over the ring. "Look how gorgeous your pearl looks on your ring."

As the pearl hovered just above the ring, I waited patiently while Mary's imagination brought the image to life.

"Mary, look at your beautiful pearl that you discovered and see how it sets so elegantly on this ring. I'm sure that you'll enjoy and remember this for the rest of your life."

"Yes, yes I love it," she conceded enthusiastically.

"Mary, it takes about two weeks to custom make your fourteen karat gold ring."

I turned Mary's hand over and lightly placed the pearl in her palm. I released her hand while her gaze remained fixed upon the pearl and reached for my pen and began to fill out an order slip. "I just need a small deposit. Would that be cash, check or credit card?"

Mary shook her head sadly. "I'd love to have it, but I'd have to pay for it with next month's rent money. My husband would kill me."

"It's entirely up to you, Mary. It's your pearl. It's your ring."

"Oh yes, I do love this ring", she sighed. "So I'll figure out a way to make sure he gets over it. Oh wait, I know," she said triumphantly. "He can skip bowling and beer with his buddies for a month and that should cover it. Okay then, I'll pay with a check."

As Mary left the room, I grabbed Matt's arm. "I cannot believe what I just saw. Mary bought that four hundred and fifty dollar ring with her rent money. This is unreal."

The ladies were in the mood and so was I. By the end of the evening, I sold the remaining two ladies including the hostess over sixteen hundred dollars in jewelry.

I mused to myself while enjoying the last glimpse of the blonde's legs as the ladies said goodbye that this could be a gold mine especially if at least ten ladies come to a 'Treasure Hunt'.

I accepted Matt's invite without hesitation to a Lumina Pearls recruitment event at the Manhattan office.


Arthur Rosen was the Executive Jeweler of the Manhattan office. He resembled the typically successful New York business man in his tailored Vicuna Italian suit and a Ralph Lauren handcrafted silk tie. Although he was short in stature, his broad shoulders bulged through the suit material indicating he must have been some kind of athlete in his youth - perhaps a wrestler, a weight lifter, or a middle linebacker who enjoyed knocking the crap out of running backs as he drilled them into the turf.

Matt introduced Rob and I to Mr. Rosen whose kind eyes greeted us warmly. But his vice grip handshake left me without a blood supply to my fingers for a few moments. Shaking the numbness out of my fingertips, I was relieved that I never had to face this guy on the football field.

Mr. Rosen guided us into the main conference room that was jam packed with anxious people. All the metal chairs were occupied and the rest of the overflow crowd were standing along the walls. Some were perusing the Lumina Pearls brochures they were supplied with when they registered for the event. Most were gazing at the stage in restless anticipation. Rob and I finally found an opening along the back wall. Standing room only! This was a very good omen.

Mr. Rosen assumed his place on stage, expanded his arms and welcomed his audience to Lumina Pearls. "Ladies and gentlemen, you are about to view a short and informative film that will demonstrate how Lumina Pearls represents an amazing opportunity to change your life."

The houselights went down and the film rolled. The Board of Directors were introduced one by one, beginning with the CEO of Lumina, Philip Imperiani, sharply attired in a custom tailored pin striped three piece suit that made him look like a million bucks or two.

"Hello and welcome to this incredible opportunity to change your life here at Lumina Pearls," Mr. Imperiani stated with absolute conviction.

The Secretary-Treasurer appeared next and the room buzzed with oohs and aahs when everyone recognized John Walters, a celebrated national television news commentator. "I have an exclusive news flash for you. Lumina Pearls will change your life!"

The energy in the room rose perceptibly with a wild chorus of 'oh yeahs' and 'right ons' and whoops flooding the room. The two co-founders and Vice Presidents of Lumina, Brad Goodman and Dennis Milton introduced themselves. They were both youthful and charismatic and their dynamic personalities leaped off the screen and aroused a wave of positive energy throughout the room where everyone was completely captivated. Mr. Milton raised his fist in a victory salute and Mr. Goodman emphatically yelled, "Are you guys ready to make some serious money!"

The crowd responded with raised fists and they roared at the top of their lungs like this was a live event and the guys in the film were actually in the room with them.

When the room quieted down a bit, Mr. Imperiani continued. "Let me introduce you to a couple of jewelers who have successfully achieved their goals." The first was an 'average' but very confident housewife who was making fifteen hundred dollars a week working as a full time Lumina jeweler. Next was a full time student at New York University majoring in graphic design. She was making one thousand dollars a week working only part time.

"Would you like to manage your own office and make a six figure salary?" asked Mr. Imperiani. Raucous cheering and foot stomping followed that question.

In the next camera shot, Mr. Imperiani stood in the center of a perfectly formed circle consisting of six brand new Cadillac Eldorado's. He spread his arms expansively. "These are the company cars you will be driving, compliments of Lumina Pearls." The prospects erupted again in a great roar.

The Cadillacs dissolved into a beautiful new house. Mr. Imperiani, with his arms still extended stood next to a Cadillac parked in the driveway. "Do you like this house?"

Like the devoted congregation at an old time religious revival, the electrified room of future Lumina Pearl jewelers responded in one voice - 'yyyyeeeeessss'.

Mr. Imperiani emphatically concluded, "We will buy you this house. There are no limits to how much money you can make."

The film ended and the hyped up crowd leaped to its feet clapping and cheering in a standing ovation. The pandemonium unified into a rhythmic beat as the frenzied prospects clapped their hands and stomped their feet as one. The walls rattled and the ceiling decorations swayed and the earthquake they created forced Arthur Rosen to take a serious look around and bolt off the stage searching for cover.


Lumina Pearls was basically a pyramid scheme patterned after the very successful Amway model. Six hundred and fifty dollars was the cost to join Lumina Pearls as a jeweler and Rob and I did not hesitate. Although I was sorely tempted to quit my job at Golden Jewelers, I continued to go through the motions at work while channeling all my energy into Lumina.

Two months went by and I was conducting three to four 'Treasure Hunts' a week. I had already signed up eight jewelers for which I received an additional ten per cent commission from their sales as well as a five percent override on any future prospects that my original jewelers enlisted.

After six months working part time, Rob and I were both earning over one thousand dollars a week and driving new Cadillacs. I did the math and shared my thoughts with Rob. "I'm making two hundred and fifty dollars a week working full time here at Golden Jewelers and doing over one thousand dollars a week running 'Treasure Hunts' part time and driving a brand new Caddy. Screw this, let's quit and go full time with Lumina."

Rob expressed his doubts. "I don't know Scott. Golden Jewelers is a steady gig and yeah, Lumina looks great right now, but what if it blows up? Then we got nothing. Sid the Sleaze would never give our jobs back to us. I just can't take that chance right now."

"You gotta do what's right for you Rob, I totally understand. But I believe this Lumina thing is a winner so the next time that weasel comes into the store, I'll tell him to get fucked right to his fat ugly face."

Two days later, I arrived at work and parked my Caddy behind Sid's beat up Ford and entered the store where the 'Sleaze' was obviously waiting for me. He was holding a roll of paper towels in one hand and a bottle of Windex in the other. Sid glanced at his watch and scowled. "You're late <u>again</u> and you didn't clean the cases before you left last night <u>again</u>." He slapped the paper towels onto my chest. "Get to work. You're lucky I don't fire your sorry ass."

"Save your bad breath, Sid." I hurled the paper towels like a Nolan Ryan fastball off Sid's chest, but he fumbled and the towels fell to the floor along with the Windex. "You're gonna have to clean the cases yourself pal because I fucking quit. By the way, do you see that new Cadillac parked behind your shit Ford? That's my new company car Sid. Have a nice life asshole."

I was now a full time Lumina Pearls jeweler. I hit the streets like a three alarm fire to recruit hostesses for my 'Treasure Hunts'. I was armed with Lumina's one hundred and fifty dollar 'Treasure Hunt' certificates that were folded over and instantly opened up like a fan with a mere flick of the wrist. Inside was an invitation to host a 'Treasure Hunt' and earn up to one hundred and fifty dollars in free jewelry. I always had at least three or four certificates ready for presentation.

I came up with a clever and very effective sales prop that was not in the Lumina training manual until they recognized that it was a great idea and made it a requirement for all Lumina jewelers. It was a clear jar with an oyster resting in salt water.

Almost every time I approached a prospect, usually a woman, the oyster in the jar would trigger an automatic question: 'What's that in the jar?'

34

With a warm smile and an enthusiastic tone I stated, "This is an oyster from Japan that contains at least one and possibly two or three cultured pearls."

The curious lady would respond, "Really, how do you know that?"

I would smile. "What is your name dear?"

"Oh, my name is Cindy."

"Hi Cindy, great to meet you. I'm Scott." I held the jar at eye level and proceeded. "This is a genuine Akoya oyster from a dedicated saltwater oyster bed in Japan, which is where the best pearls in the world come from. And the pearls inside here were cultivated over a period of four years which guarantees their beauty and authenticity. Cindy, have you ever attended a Lumina Pearls 'Treasure Hunt'?"

"No, what's it all about?"

"It's an exciting event that is hosted by ladies like yourself in their own home. They invite their friends over for a 'Treasure Hunt' where they pluck oysters, one by one, and discover a cultured pearl or two in every oyster. Then they have the option to mount their beautiful pearl or pearls, depending on how many they discover, in a gorgeous fourteen karat gold custom made jewelry piece direct from the manufacturer at wholesale prices."

Cindy shakes her head in disbelief. "That sounds like a Tupperware or an Amway party."

"It's not a party Cindy, it's an exciting 'Treasure Hunt'. I'm sure you've never seen anything like it. As the hostess, you can earn up to one hundred and fifty dollars in free fourteen karat gold jewelry. Do you have any friends who might be interested in hosting a 'Treasure Hunt'?"

Most of the time they would express interest in hosting their own 'Treasure Hunt' and I would whip out the certificate, flick my wrist and fan it open almost like a magic trick. "Here is how we're going to get that one hundred and fifty dollars in free jewelry. The first thing I'm going to do is give you a complimentary oyster that is guaranteed to have at least one genuine cultured pearl.

All the other ladies will pay five dollars per oyster with the same pearl guarantee in every oyster. Next, I will give you two dollars in free jewelry for every lady that shows up whether she buys anything or not, so if twenty ladies show up, you have forty dollars in free jewelry right away.

Hold on, there's more coming. I'll give you three dollars in free jewelry for each piece of jewelry that is purchased and believe me, the ladies love the jewelry and most of them will buy at least one piece. For example, if fifteen pieces are purchased, that's another forty five dollars in free jewelry.

Now if one of your friends book their own 'Treasure Hunt', you will receive an additional ten dollars in free jewelry. If two friends sign up to host, it will be an additional fifteen dollars, and you'll love this, if a third friend makes a booking, I will give you an extra thirty dollars, that's a total of fifty five dollars for three bookings, and Cindy, if you get ten of your friends to show up, I always guarantee that my hostesses will have the three bookings.

Cindy, I want you to be completely comfortable with hosting the 'Treasure Hunt' so I will come to your house two weeks before the actual event with invitations, envelopes and stamps and explain to you exactly when to mail your invitations which is very important. For every return envelope that comes back to you in the mail, I will give you another dollar in free jewelry so twenty envelopes would be another twenty dollars. Invite all your friends, relatives and whoever else comes to mind and leave the rest to me."

My full time dedication to Lumina Pearls resulted in a phenomenal 'Treasure Hunt' record of running at least one 'Treasure Hunt' a day for fifty five consecutive days. My incredible performance caught the eyes of the Lumina Pearls Board of Directors.

Dennis Milton, the energetic Lumina Vice President featured in the recruitment film, surprised me with a phone call congratulating me for my remarkable success and offering to promote me to an 'executive jeweler' position. "Our business is expanding like crazy and we're opening offices all over the country. This is an opportunity for you to manage your own office. At this point, we're not sure in which city you'll be opening an office, but we need you to come out here to Lumina Pearls National Headquarters in Beverly Hills to train for thirty days."

I couldn't believe what I was hearing. I sincerely thanked Mr. Milton and assured him that I would love to become an 'executive jeweler'. Then I paused and reflected how nice it would be to take a little time off before heading out West to start my new life. Let's see, today is Wednesday. This is great. I can relax and enjoy an extra long weekend.

"When would you like me to be there?"

"We want you out here in Beverly Hills bright and early on Monday morning," Milton said matter of factly.

I almost fell over. Damn. There goes my long weekend. I composed myself and told him I'd book a flight and be there by Sunday.

"Forget the flight Scott. We want you to drive your company car out here. You're going to need it during your training and also in the new city where you'll open your first office."

"But, Mr. Milton, it's three thousand miles from New York to Beverly Hills. Today is Wednesday. There's no way I can be there by Monday morning."

"No problem, Scott. You have a new Cadillac, right? Hit the road early tomorrow and we'll see you on Monday!"

I did the calculations in my head. If I leave tomorrow morning, that's Thursday, I'll have four days to cover three thousand miles, so that would be about seven hundred fifty miles a day. Hell's bells man, how will I stay awake? I'll need a shitload of diet pills to do this. No problem, I'll just grab some from my neighbor, Ralph, who always has a larger inventory than most pharmacies.

Later that evening, I had dinner with my girlfriend Amy at a nice Italian place. I knew she wouldn't take the news well so I was fairly confident with the idea that I had selected an upscale restaurant to preclude any public displays of hysteria. However, when I rationally explained the job opportunity in Beverly Hills, she instantly became hysterical.

"I'll never see you again. You'll forget me. Everyone knows what goes on in California and you'll be right next door to Hollywood. That place is full of nothing but whores and drug dealers. I can't believe this is happening."

Even though I promised I'd send her a plane ticket in a month and that we'd be together again in a new city, the tears were flowing like a waterfall. Amy was an inconsolable mess and it wasn't long before the restaurant manager politely asked us to leave.

As I got in my car to go home and pack, my mind was already on the expressway dreading the three thousand mile car trip from hell wondering how I was going to beat the ticking clock and make it to Beverly Hills on time.

# Chapter Three

## DON'T SHIT WHERE YOU EAT

My 1975 Cadillac El Dorado, also known as the 'Beast', had a generous fuel capacity of twenty seven gallons, but the catch was the gas mileage - a pitiful nine miles to the gallon which meant stopping for gas every two hundred thirty miles or so. I left New York City early on Thursday morning on Interstate 75 West and two hundred and thirty one miles later I was forced to make my first stop to refuel the 'Beast' in the town of Burnt Cabins, Pennsylvania.

From there, I was hoping to make it to Zanesville, Ohio for the next gas stop, but the fuel gauge needle was buried deep in the red zone with more than fifty miles to go. Fortunately, I spotted a solitary gas pump by the side of the road in the middle of nowhere. There were a few double wide trailers scattered throughout what seemed to be a graveyard of dozens of old rusty vehicles that were scattered, helter skelter, across the barren countryside.

A strange looking guy who I hoped was the attendant sauntered out of the shack that functioned as the office stuffing his face with chips with one hand and brushing the crumbs off his dirty oil splotched denim coveralls with the other. "What can I do you for?"

"Fill 'er up with Supreme."

The attendant grabbed the handle of the gas hose, set the bag of chips on the trunk, unscrewed the gas cap and paused. He was holding the gas handle in midair and his gaze was locked on the back window of the Caddy, a cloud of disgust was covering his face.

"Everything okay?" I asked cautiously.

He shook his head and continued to stare straight ahead. "I can't believe what I'm seeing here, mister."

"What exactly are you looking at?"

"Are you some kind of New York Yankee fan?" nodding to the decal on the back window of the 'Beast'.

"Well yeah," I replied carefully, "as you can see I'm from New York."

"You're not in New York anymore, mister, and we don't much care for the Yankees around here."

"I mean no offense, what did you say your name was?"

He tapped the name tag on his soiled work shirt which read 'Elroy'.

"Okay Elroy, my name is Scott and I understand how you feel. I just need some gas and I'll be on my way."

"I don't know, mister, it ain't right to be aiding and abetting no Yankee fan."

"Here's twenty dollars for the gas, Elroy, and another twenty for your trouble."

"Are you trying to bribe an honest man?"

"No, not at all Elroy. Think of it as a tip for doing a fine job."

I stuffed the bills in Elroy's shirt pocket before he could object again. "I'm gonna grab a soda Elroy, I'll get one for you too."

Elroy was placing the gas handle back in the pump when I returned and gave him the soda which he accepted without a word. I didn't breathe a sigh of relief until I was back on the road.

A few miles later, I pulled over and scraped the Yankee sticker off the window and gave some thought to ditching the New York license plates. Damn, I'll have to drive like a saint and stay five or ten miles under the posted speed limit the rest of the way. This long road trip was already getting longer.

It was time to pop a couple of diet pills to power me through the night. Soon enough they kicked in and I was a rabid ball of

43

energy, chewing up some serious mileage, rocking down the road to the thunderous sounds of AC/DC. Little did I know, I was literally on the 'Highway to Hell'. Not much later, my head exploded into hot flashes and waves of nausea rolled through my stomach. I was crawling out of my skin with claustrophobia as the sides of the 'Beast' closed in on me.

Screw the speed limit, I had to cool off somehow. The speedometer rocketed to almost ninety. I rolled down the window and stuck my head out and panted like a dog. The force of the wind peeled my face back, but somehow it actually felt good and the heat that consumed my body began to abate. I eased my head back inside the car and assumed a normal driving position but my hands were all cramped up and I could not unwrap my fingers from their iron grip on the steering wheel to shift the 'Beast' down to a lower gear and slow down. Jesus H. Christ, what the hell is happening here?

My neighbor Ralph forgot to mention that these goddamn pills had some serious side effects like paralysis and hallucinations, but then he probably never took them four or five at a time. I savored a brief moment of respite as my paranoia subsided, but the frenetic buzz in my brain did not let up. I sucked in the cool air of relief and slowly exhaled. The golden sun was setting against the pale blue sky. My reverie was shattered by row after row of oncoming headlights that frantically flashed off and on. Was there something wrong with my car or my driving? I checked all the dashboard gauges and they were normal so I put the pedal to the metal again and vowed to press on through the night.

But then the tempo of the song on the radio slowed down and Mick Jagger began slurring his words while the guitars became horribly distorted. I figured it was just a weak radio signal. I must be getting out of range. On its own, the radio volume surged and my ears exploded in excruciating pain. I saw three radio dials dancing in opposing directions and I couldn't figure out which one to touch to lower the volume.

I concentrated again on the road only to be assaulted by a shimmering barrage of fiery yellow suns that refused to drop below the horizon. I blinked furiously and tears flowed freely from my eyes that could no longer focus. The crescendo of blaring car horns slowly faded away only to swell into another wave of cacophony.

The 'Beast' seemed to have a mind of its own and began to spin in slow motion. The orgy of sweltering suns surrounded me and were soon eclipsed by a ring of dirty brown clouds and menacing green leaves slapping against the windshield. Then the world completely stopped. I sat in the eerie silence and checked to insure my body parts were still intact. I carefully opened the door and tentatively set one foot on the ground. Okay, it was solid. But the front end of my Caddy was buried in a crush of giant corn stalks at the edge of some farmer's field of corn.

I sat down and leaned back against the 'Beast' and waited for the horizon to stop spinning. I opened my eyes and noticed the red tail lights of the cars passing by on the road had reversed course and were streaming back towards me in bursts of strobe light intensity. I closed my eyes. Oh god please, when will this shit end?

I resigned myself to whatever the fates had in store for me when a torrent of unrelenting fever like heat swept through my body. I was flooded with rivers of sweat. My clothes were drenched. I had been baptized in my own sweat. Somehow I felt better but I had no idea how long I had been in that cornfield.

I got back in the 'Beast' and vowed to soldier on through the night. Late Friday afternoon, I rolled into Oklahoma City, stopped at the first motel and left a wake up call for midnight. That would be six hours of sleep, but evidently I fell into a coma and didn't hear a damn thing. Twelve hours later at six a.m. Saturday morning, the sun filled the hotel room with harsh light and I slowly opened my eyes.

I glanced at my watch and panicked for a moment. I needed to hit Rifle, Colorado by the end of the day. I considered popping only one diet pill for about a second and a half, but there was no fucking way I was going through that hallucination shit again. Instead, I opted for another popular drug, caffeine. I probably drank twenty cups of coffee that day and the only side effect was occasionally vibrating and shaking more than the car engine.

The caffeine had worn off by the time I checked into yet another 'economy' motel and was sound asleep before I hit the lumpy mattress. It was Saturday night in Rifle and I believe I was the only non resident of the town checked into the motel. There was a wife beater in the room on one side of me and a vine swinging ape-man who was fucking a screaming hyena on the other side. The town drunks were gathered in the parking lot just outside my door singing their favorite songs out of tune and at full volume. I prayed dear god, this can't go on all night. But it did.

I gave up and left Rifle at two a.m. for the last leg of the trip, roughly thirteen hours to Beverly Hills. I spent the first two hours on the road debating with myself the merits of taking only half a diet pill. Okay, how about a quarter of a pill, that's a fair compromise right? Ah, the hell with pills. I rolled down all the windows and let the cold night air freeze my eyelids wide open.

The Sunday morning sun slowly rose behind me and I decided the drug of the day would again be caffeine. I pulled into a truck stop jammed with eighteen wheelers, found one of the last parking spots and joined my fellow road warriors in the diner for some coffee.

My nose was buried in the menu when a friendly female voice asked me if I'd like some coffee. Without the hallucinogenic benefit of a diet pill, I swear Ellie Mae Clampett from the Beverly Hillbillies was standing behind the counter asking me that question. Oh yes please, I smiled. She asked if I'd like anything to go with that and I fantasized - 'yeah baby, how about you' - just like every other rowdy, red-blooded cowboy in the place.

She leaned over the counter and asked, "Haven't I seen you before, like on TV or maybe in the movies?"

"No not me," I replied tapping the menu. "Are there any specials today?"

"Well there ain't no specials on the menu, but if you're interested," she leaned in closer and winked. "I sure could whip you up something special during my lunch break later on."

As much as I love the Rolling Stones, 'time was not on my side' that day. I had to get back on the torturous road and this dilemma was killing me in more ways than one. After my tenth cup of coffee, I limped out of the diner and circled the parking lot trying like hell to walk off my woody before I got back in my car. It took a couple of hours of determined driving to finally defeat the sweet temptation of turning around and heading back to the diner for the 'lunch break special'.

I thought I won the battle with myself until I saw the beckoning hotel/casinos of Sin City even though it was broad daylight. Somehow I managed to muster up the willpower to drive straight through the heart of Las Vegas without stopping to indulge in the vast array of entertainment possibilities including strip joints that never closed. Instead I plunged into the endless expanse of the Mojave Desert to endure the last few hours of this horrendous road trip to Beverly Hills, California.

The last of the caffeine was wearing off as I stopped in the valet service lane of the Beverly Hilton. I could only think about the wonderful night's sleep that was only minutes away. However, just as I lay my head down on the pillow the room phone rang. "Welcome to Beverly Hills," boomed the friendly voice of Dennis

Milton. "Meet me in the lobby in thirty minutes, we're going out to dinner. What do you prefer? Italian, French, Mexican?"

"Something light, like sushi," I managed to reply, fighting off the tsunami wave of fatigue that flooded me.

"Japanese it is," Mr. Milton confirmed and clicked off the call.

Then I heard another voice in the room. It was my own. The one in my head suggesting the only way I could stay awake was… oh no, not a diet pill. Fortunately, I won that argument with myself and somehow tapped into an energy source often called 'mind over matter'. I quickly dressed and headed to the lobby.

After detailing the highlights of Southern California, Mr. Milton sang the praises of Lumina and emphasized the tremendous opportunities for personal wealth that the company represented. Hard work was richly rewarded, he stressed, and he had no doubt that I would be incredibly successful. He raised his glass and wished me a long and successful venture with Lumina. I went to bed that night full of good vibes and confidence that tomorrow would be the first day of a remarkable career.

The next morning when I arrived at Lumina Headquarters on Sepulveda Boulevard and saw BMW's and Mercedes's dominating the parking lot, my decision to roll the dice with Lumina was confirmed.

The building was a beautiful classic Spanish style two story structure with glistening white adobe walls complimented by a traditional red tile roof and surrounded by tall graceful palm trees moving gently in the soft ocean breeze.

I passed through the massive oak doorway into the lobby where my laser sharp eyes immediately focused on the stunning receptionist. Her iridescent green eyes met mine and momentarily rendered me speechless. I quickly recovered and marveled at the temporary paralyzing impact that a beautiful woman can have on an unsuspecting man.

"Good morning. I'm Scott Newman, here to see Dennis Milton. What's your name?"

"Oh hi, Mr. Newman, I'm Jessie. So nice to meet you. Everyone is expecting you in the Board Room. Right this way."

Where have I seen a perfect booty like that before, I mused. Oh yeah, the blonde in the black mini skirt at my first 'Treasure Hunt'. For a moment, I entertained the oyster fantasy that popped into my head, but quickly deleted that thought.

Back to reality, Mr. Milton greeted me warmly at the door. I entered the Board Room and was welcomed by all the Lumina luminaries I had viewed in the recruitment film at every weekly Lumina Open House in New York for the past three months. I knew that film better than the original editor and director. And there I was, sitting among the kingpins of the company in a richly appointed conference room that reeked of success.

Mr. Imperiani called the meeting to order and mentioned to me that every Monday morning at nine o'clock sharp, the Board Members convened here at Lumina Headquarters to review the

50

previous week and plan for the present week and their future events. And of course, to introduce the newest candidate for the position of 'Executive Jeweler'.

"Mr. Newman," continued Mr. 'I', as he preferred to be called, "you are far and away the best salesman we've seen in the history of Lumina Pearls. Not only did you set a record of conducting 'Treasure Hunts' for fifty five consecutive days that will never be broken, but you also introduced a very unique marketing concept: a genuine oyster elegantly displayed in a clear glass container of sea water. This simple yet effective marketing tool persuaded countless prospective women to become 'Treasure Hunt' hostesses. Our jewelry sales have increased substantially and this practical approach is now featured in our training manuals and required in all training sessions.

We applaud you for your outstanding performance and anticipate that at some point in the near future, you will be appointed to a 'Regional Executive Jeweler' position. You will have a minimum of six 'Executive Jeweler Offices' under your jurisdiction and that guarantees a six figure salary plus overrides on all jewelry sales from those offices. There will be only four 'Regional' positions available. We have big plans for you, Mr. Newman. Your thirty day training period will begin with a week here at our headquarters followed by three weeks as the 'Head Executive Jeweler' at our company owned Riverside office. After successfully completing the training period, you may select a city to open your own office from a number of options located throughout the country."

I looked around the room at the smiling faces with quiet confidence as the meeting adjourned. I was absolutely certain that someday I would be sitting at that table as a Member of the Lumina Board.

Mr. Milton escorted me to his private office to commence my Lumina training. "Mr. Newman," he began somberly. "Working for Lumina Pearls is a privilege that all of us take very seriously. We have a stellar reputation to uphold and that requires a personal code of conduct for all of us here in the Lumina family. I'm going to be totally straight with you and not pull any punches or sugar coat anything. We don't shit where we eat."

Milton paused to let his words sink in. When he figured I had fully absorbed the depth of that profound statement he proceeded. "Look, Mr. Newman. You're a handsome and charming guy from the 'Big Apple' and the ladies out here go nuts over East Coast men, especially New Yorkers. Sure, you can have your pick of the litter of all these lovely young jewelers who are always ready to rock, but we're here to work not screw around with the help, okay?"

"Of course, Mr. Milton, I understand," I nodded soberly.

"Even though we happen to be situated next to Hollywood, do not mistake Lumina Pearls for the film industry where it's normal for those guys to screw everything that moves. We don't have casting calls or make movies or TV shows so we actually have standards and high ones at that.

Just keep in mind that you're in a position of leadership and you have the responsibility of training and guiding these impressionable ladies. Always remember that you're a professional and you represent the hard earned reputation of Lumina where we never mix business with pleasure. Keep your dick in your pants."

"Mr. Milton, I want to assure you that I am completely focused on this incredible opportunity you've given me and there is no way I'd mess it up like that. I have a steady girlfriend back home in New York and we're planning to marry after I have my own office in a new city. And then we can start thinking about a family."

Milton held up his hand. "Forgive me for coming on so strong, but as you can see, I'm very passionate about our company and sometimes I get a little carried away. I'm just looking out for your best interests. I trust that you understand, Mr. Newman?"

"No worries, Mr. Milton. I appreciate your honesty and give you my word that my conduct will always be honorable." And thanks for the inspirational sermon.

At the end of that long day, Reverend Milton invited me to dinner where I met his rather plain looking, live-in girlfriend, Stella. Brad Goodman and his dumpy, jewelry laden wife were also in attendance. I was thankful for the presence of the ladies so there would be no morality lectures from the good Reverend. I survived the dinner and retreated to my room to study the two inch thick 'training' manual.

The week of training went by quickly and I wanted to celebrate and treat myself to a fabulous dinner at the revolving restaurant at the top of the Hollywood Holiday Inn that I had heard so much about. 'Five Stars' only began to describe the spectacular view of Hollywood's twinkling lights spread like a magic carpet all the way to the Pacific Ocean.

The restaurant had a cylindrical shape; a perfect circle rotating slowly forty stories high. There was a bar occupying the center and two concentric circles of dining tables moving in opposing directions. The outer ring of tables was situated next to the floor to ceiling windows and featured a commanding aerial view of the shimmering full moon Hollywood night.

I was seated at a table in the inner ring surrounding the bar scanning the menu when Jessie, the gorgeous receptionist, suddenly appeared directly in front of me. She was seated at a table in the outer ring that was slowly moving past me. Her hand rested casually on the lap of the Reverend himself, Dennis Milton.

I could not believe my eyes. Across the table from Milton and Jessie was Brad Goodman cozied up with an older attractive female, definitely not his wife. Where had I seen her before? My mind raced through my memory bank and - holy shit! She was the 'average' housewife in the Lumina recruitment film allegedly making fifteen hundred dollars a week. There was nothing average about her tonight. Perfect hair and makeup, sexy low cut dress, fondling Goodman like they were long time lovers.

'Don't shit where you eat?' Yeah, right you are Reverend. I watched intently from behind my menu as their table passed by. Okay Milton, you lying sack of shit, I was right about you the first time we met. You shoulda been a TV evangelist. Most of them end up getting busted as a bunch of horny, two-faced hypocrites too. I was fairly certain that even the local porn stars could learn a thing or two from the Reverend and his bedroom shenanigans that would take place later on that night.

A couple of days later I was having lunch with the Reverend in the company cafeteria when I spotted a sensational looking redhead walking toward our table. What is it about mini skirts that just kills me. Hopefully, Milton couldn't read my mind so I could avoid another sermon. To my surprise and delight, she stopped at our table.

She offered her hand to me and said, "You must be Scott Newman."

I took her hand and was again surprised when she did not release her grip. "Yes, I am. And you are?"

"Heidi Palmer. I've heard so many great things about you. Rumor has it that you are going to be the 'Executive Jeweler' at the Riverside office. That's my home office so I'm really looking forward to learning a few tricks of the trade from the master."

"I'm flattered Heidi. I hope to live up to such high expectations. So nice to meet you and I'll see you soon."

Milton was staring at our lingering handshake so I knew the dreaded sermon was inevitable. "Mr. Newman, remember our conversation about mixing business with pleasure. Hey, we're all human, right? And we are constantly surrounded by temptations. Just enjoy the view, and then let those tempting thoughts go."

You're absolutely right, Reverend Milton, but what happens if those tempting thoughts come back when I see her again?

Southern California is essentially a vast expanse of desert sand ironically situated next to the endless blue waters of the Pacific Ocean. Riverside, however, is located in the middle of this desert and nowhere near the ocean. I settled into my new office and began the preparations for the training of forty future Lumina jewelers. Oh well, I guess there aren't any distractions in this godforsaken town.

Tap, tap, tap. I looked up and there was a gorgeous redhead standing coyly in the doorway holding a tray of breakfast items. "Hi Mr. Newman, remember me, Heidi Palmer? I brought you some coffee and donuts."

"Heidi! Great to see you again. Thank you so much," I said, relieving her of the tray.

"Just to let you know, Riverside is my home town and I'd be happy to show you around. What are you doing for dinner tonight? I know where the corporate apartment is so I'll pick you up at seven."

She left with a wink before I could say a word.

Promptly at seven, Heidi rolled up in a classic convertible 1967 silver blue Corvette. She cat walked deliberately up the sidewalk modeling her magnificent fanny in a black mini skirt perfectly accented with killer stilettos. How do all of these women know my greatest weakness? I tried not to stare at her fabulous body parts all through dinner. I failed on purpose.

After dinner and back in the Corvette, we were cruising through the manicured grounds of an exclusive country club and I was marveling at the private estates of architectural masterpieces when she turned into the driveway of a majestic Spanish Colonial villa. This couldn't be Riverside. Certainly, we were in the heart of the enchanting Tuscany Valley region of Italy.

"Would you care for a night cap," she asked demurely. She didn't wait for a response and the massive wrought iron gate automatically opened onto a spacious circular drive consisting of muted red adobe brick. A garden of lush red Geraniums formed the perimeter of the entire driveway. The classic Mediterranean two story home featured white stucco walls, red clay terra cotta roof tiles and a hand crafted staircase winding up to a grand balcony.

What the hell is the deal with this woman, I wondered. This can't be her home. Maybe she knows the people who live here. We passed through the double oak doors and entered a stunning open area perfectly appointed with warm, dark wood furniture on a white tile floor accented by a colorful mosaic design. White sand textured walls ascended to an exceptionally high ceiling of rustic wooden beams.

There were paintings of Degas and Renoir featuring exquisite ballerinas and beautiful nudes. I was overwhelmed by Heidi's uncanny resemblance to Gustav Klint's erotic and mysterious portrayals of his alluring female subject.

My mind was spinning. She seems to be living in a world that I am not remotely familiar with. Why is she posing as a Lumina Jeweler when she was probably the model for Klint's incredible art work? No that's not possible, or is it? Is this really happening or just a psychedelic side effect from overdosing on the diet pills?

She asked me to make a couple of drinks and excused herself. Moments later, she was standing in an archway wearing an incredibly revealing Victoria's Secret negligee. She drew closer to me and before I could utter a word, the negligee floated to the floor. My hands were guided by hers onto her soft and warm breasts and she whispered in my ear 'follow me'.

Three weeks of training new jewelers went by fast. Three weeks of Heidi went by even faster. I never solved the mystery of that woman or the mansion. Did she have a husband who was never around? Did she inherit it? Was she the interior designer or was she just the maid? Maybe she just had the key.

I returned to the Beverly Hills Headquarters and selected St. Louis as the city for my new office as an 'Executive Jeweler'. The Board wanted me to remain in Beverly Hills for an additional two weeks of training and of course, the Reverend would be my mentor again.

Milton wasted no time. "So Mr. Newman, I understand that Heidi Palmer was one of your jewelers. How did that go?"

How do you think it went you fucking hypocrite?

"I behaved like a professional, Mr. Milton. I observed the Lumina Pearls code of conduct to the letter."

"I'm relieved to hear that, Mr. Newman, but certainly you were tempted?"

"Of course I was, but like you said, business comes first and there is no way I was going to jeopardize this fantastic opportunity."

Milton slowly nodded, but his eyes told me that he didn't believe a word I said. I continued to see Heidi every night for the next two weeks right under Pinocchio's nose.

After three weeks of frolicking with Heidi, no, make that five weeks, I was severely exhausted and sleep deprived as I began my long drive to St. Louis. Luckily, I still had some diet pills from the previous nightmare journey across the country. So I compromised and I only popped half a pill every eight hours to avoid any hallucinogenic complications.

Before I left Beverly Hills, I made sure to scrape off the ridiculous Los Angeles Dodger baseball decal that some asshole pasted in the same spot on my rear window where the New York Yankee sticker had been prominently featured. These are two of the most hated teams in baseball (OK three if you count Boston) and I didn't need any more shit from a guy named Elroy or one of his West Coast cousins.

I rolled into St. Louis with an iron determination to insure my new office would be a smashing success. I quickly leased an apartment and found an adequate space for my new office in an excellent downtown location. I had stalled for a week before flying Amy to St. Louis mainly to recover my stamina from the Heidi adventure. No doubt Amy would immediately jump my bones to make up for lost time.

Within six weeks, I had trained an energetic work force of fifty jewelers and the 'Treasure Hunts' were yielding healthy commissions from the jewelry sales. Things were looking very promising at the St. Louis office except for a couple lingering problems that eventually proved to be catastrophic.

I had paid the hefty seven thousand five hundred dollar fee to Lumina Headquarters to open my new office, but they had not reimbursed me for the security deposit or the first two months of the office lease. They were also seriously behind in paying commissions on the jewelry sales. After several phone calls which escalated into anger and threats on my part, Lumina would finally throw me a bone, but this pattern would only get worse.

On the domestic front, Amy's mother had refused to allow her to leave New York unless she promised to get married to me the second she arrived in St. Louis. "My daughter won't be living in sin, especially with that scoundrel." Like an incurable rash, her mother would not go away. She harassed and hounded Amy every day. "I want to see a marriage license. Don't keep putting it off. I want to see that legal piece of paper now!"

Amy in turn, hounded me every single day. The tipping point came when her mother gave us a deadline of one week. If a copy of the marriage license was not in her mail box within the week, she would get on a plane and execute her own version of a 'shotgun' wedding when she arrived. The day after she issued the threat, we were married by a Justice of the Peace during my lunch hour.

After four consecutive months of achieving the top sales volume of all the offices in the country, Amy and I were invited to Beverly Hills for a grand Lumina celebration to recognize the top 'Executive Jewelers'. Lumina flew us first class and put us up in a suite at the Beverly Hilton in Beverly Hills. Although I appreciated the accolades and the impressive company 'perks', I was becoming more and more angry and disenchanted with their business practices. How the hell could they hemorrhage cash on travel, accommodations and lavish party expenses for this bullshit 'perk' and leave me up shit creek with all the basic office expenses.

The board members were making the grand social rounds with their trophy wives on their arms. Reverend Milton was perfectly coifed and dressed to the nines in an immaculate tuxedo. I thought he would look even better after I shoved him into the swimming pool. Perhaps he sensed my intentions and managed to avoid me the entire evening. But Heidi Palmer did not.

"Hi Mr. Newman, so nice to see you again."

Of course she was wearing an amazing mini skirt which brought back some rousing memories I quickly repressed.

"Heidi, great to see you too."

"This must be your lovely wife. I'm Heidi Palmer. Your husband was the 'Executive Jeweler' I worked under and I can't begin to tell you how much I learned from him. He's the best instructor I've ever experienced. I could go on all night so I'll just say it was great to see you again, Mr. Newman, and lovely to meet you Amy. You're a lucky lady."

Whoa, I dodged that bullet. I just hoped there were no more coming in my direction at least for the remainder of the evening.

We were scheduled to fly out on Sunday, but I changed the flight so I could drop by the Monday morning Board Meeting to get some straight answers. There was a new receptionist who informed me that it was a closed session and the Board Members were not to be disturbed. That's okay, just let them know Scott Newman is here and there won't be a problem.

The door opened and the Reverend greeted me like a long lost parishioner. I glanced back at the gorgeous secretary and figured he was already screwing her too. Mr. 'I' expanded his arms just like he did in the recruitment film when he presented the company Cadillacs to all of us suckers. "Mr. Newman, so great to see you again so soon. How did you enjoy the party?"

"I had a good time Mr. 'I', thank you for your hospitality. Now if you don't mind, I have some concerns that I hope all of you can address because no one seems to be answering their fucking phones so I'd appreciate some straight answers."

Brad Goodman jumped in with his smooth, condescending voice oozing with false charm. "Mr. Newman, we're expanding like crazy. We are opening offices all over the country which ultimately benefits you. You need to be just a little more patient and once things settle down and Lumina is operating in full gear, we'll take care of you in spades."

"Well, Mr. Goodman, I need to be taken care of right now. You have not paid my office rent for three months. You're behind in sales commissions to my jewelers and I'm not receiving any overrides from the Chesterfield office I helped Mr. and Mrs. Whitehall open. I worked my ass off setting up that office. I traveled there every damn weekend for over a month training thirty jewelers.

I originally recruited the Whitehalls and encouraged them to become 'Executive Jewelers' and now I look like an asshole because you won't cover their expenses. I am not going to bullshit them like you're bullshitting me."

"Relax Mr. Newman," advised Mr. 'I'. "Think of this as just a small bump in the road. I assure you that we will be up to speed in the short term."

I couldn't believe these arrogant assholes. They sat there like kings expecting me to be grateful for their bullshit promises of a few crumbs they may or may not throw me. But I knew they had to play nice and tolerate me for a few more minutes before they got back to counting the mountains of money that I made for them. They sure as hell were not going to fire their number one revenue producer.

I returned to St. Louis and nothing changed. I continued paying commissions to my jewelers out of my own pocket until Lumina's inconsistent payments came to a complete halt. I was already in debt from paying the monthly office lease when the memo arrived that proved to be the last straw. It simply stated that Lumina had eliminated 'overrides' to 'Executive Jewelers'. The pyramid had completely collapsed along with my patience with these blowhard scumbags.

I didn't need any damn diet pills to drive the 'Beast' from St. Louis straight through to Beverly Hills. I arrived early Monday morning and waited in the Lumina parking lot until a few minutes after nine o'clock so the Board meeting would be well under way. I wanted to make sure those conniving thieves were sitting comfortably in their Boardroom chairs around the Boardroom conference table.

I fired up the 'Beast', revved the engine and raced around the parking lot like Bobby Unser. The tires were screeching and the engine was raging as I suddenly hit the brakes and screamed to a halt right in front of the huge board room picture window. I was close enough to see their eyes and mouths growing larger and larger especially when they recognized that the driver was Scott Newman.

I slammed the gears into reverse and burned rubber backwards across the parking lot, then shifted into 'drive' and thundered directly toward the window. I knew they would shit their pants and hit the floor. At the last second, I slammed on the brakes and continued to press the gas pedal to the floor. The rear tires were screeching and digging into the pavement. Clouds of ugly black smoke filled the air as I alternated between pressing the brakes and the gas pedal forcing the rear end of the 'Beast' to swing around in a 360 degree circle, a driving technique known as 'spinning a donut'.

I spun two complete 'donuts' then stopped to admire the thick, black cloud of smoke as it slowly dissipated. When the view was clear again, I performed a series of stuttering starts and stops as the car lurched toward the window. At the last second, I released the brakes, hit the gas, and veered just to the left of the window and smashed the front end of the 'Beast' into the wall.

Steam sprayed like a fountain and white smoke spewed from the mangled radiator. I unbuckled my seat belt, removed the keys from the ignition and stood in front of the Board Room window holding the Caddy keys high above my head. The Board Members were cautiously collecting themselves from the floor and staring wide eyed at the crumpled 'Beast' and then back at me.

I slapped the car keys against the huge picture window and stuck them there with a piece of tape. I turned away from the terrified faces, bent over, slipped my pants over my lily white ass and mooned those pompous douchebags. I did not look back as I walked to the taxi that was waiting for me at the entrance of the vainglorious Beverly Hills Headquarters of Lumina Pearls.

# Chapter Four

## CHRISTMAS IN JULY

Amy and I returned to New York and settled back into our old familiar neighborhood. Because of my jewelry background and sales ability, I quickly landed a job with Litton Jewelers managing one of their six stores for a lousy four hundred dollars a week. Of course, they gave me the shittiest store in the worst location with the worst sales record. I rolled up my sleeves and attacked the challenge with my typical unlimited supply of energy and my bulletproof positive attitude. Within just a few months, my store was kicking ass. We rocketed from the weakest sales record of the six stores to the best.

The Litton owners couldn't figure it out. How did I achieve this phenomenal revenue upswing in a damn near ghetto location with no parking lot? How did I top the number one store situated in a beautiful mall in a prime location? Those advantages were unbelievable: tons of parking, trendy shops and boutiques, snack kiosks and upscale restaurants. It was a Yuppie shopping paradise. But the answer to my success was simple. First, I persuaded the Littons to stock my store with the same high quality inventory the other five shops carried. Next, I hired a well-trained professional sales staff and cultivated excellent customer relations. I implemented effective promotion and marketing strategies that attracted loyal customers and kept them coming back. I believed this generated positive 'word of mouth' which I never underestimated or ignored.

Maria Alvarez was my best salesperson and also the most attractive. She looked like Marilyn Monroe with wavy dark hair. Every male customer who entered the store seemed to be magnetically drawn to her. Female customers were equally enchanted by her natural charisma. There was never a hint of sales pressure from her. She possessed the rare quality of making people feel at ease and genuinely welcome. No one ever felt like they were just another customer. Most folks left the store with the uplifting feeling akin to a delightful rendezvous with a friend (and the beautiful piece of jewelry she casually suggested).

One evening after work, Amy and I were walking through an upscale fashion square after enjoying a wonderful dinner. There were a variety of trendy shops including a clothing boutique, optical store, high end women's shoe shop and a furrier. I was wondering why I hadn't seen any jewelry stores when I noticed an empty store front in a corner location with a 'For Lease' sign in the window. It was the only empty shop in the entire fashion square. Boom! The idea hit me like a bolt of lightning and I eagerly shared it with Amy.

"We're going to open our own jewelry store right here and call it 'Scott Newman Jewelers'!"

"You are completely out of your mind," Amy protested. "You just can't bounce from a jewelry store manager to a jewelry store owner overnight. Look around Scott, this is a high class fashion square. We have no money for something like this. They wouldn't rent a space to you in a million years. Come back to earth, Scott. This is only a crazy dream."

"You're right honey. Today it's only a crazy dream, but tomorrow is when I begin working my ass off to make it a reality." I gently held her shoulders and turned her to face the spacious window of the empty shop. "Take a good look and use your imagination. I see a magnificent jewelry store, don't you? I want you to see what I see and work with me to make it happen. We can do this!"

The next morning, I called the number for the lease and made an appointment with Roger Elias, the manager of the fashion square property. "Mr. Elias," I said looking him right in the eyes. "You don't know me, but I can make you a pile of money. I would like to open a jewelry store that I guarantee will substantially increase your fashion square traffic like you cannot imagine. I have plenty of experience in the jewelry business and I am the best sales and marketing guy you will ever run into."

I explained in great detail my idea of an elegant store with mid to high end jewelry at prices so aggressive that customers would have to line up to get in the shop.

"Mr. Elias, my promotional plans will benefit the entire fashion square with huge numbers of customers. If you just give me a chance, I promise you won't regret your decision. What do you have to lose?"

Mr. Elias leaned forward in his chair and looked directly at me. "Mr. Newman, I'll be honest with you. Any other time, I would have politely shown anyone as undercapitalized as you to the door. However, I am so impressed with your determination and confidence and so intrigued with your plan that I am going to think it over and get back to you. Fair enough?"

"Thank you, Mr. Elias. I promise I won't let you down," I assured him.

Amy was waiting for me at home with her 'I told you so' smirk already on her face.

"He didn't say no," I said. "The door is still open and I have a very good feeling about this."

She crossed her arms and just shook her head. Three days later I signed the lease. I should have called 911 before I told Amy the good news because she almost passed out.

I proceeded to plunge into serious debt to make this dream a reality. I maxed out all my credit cards, took out personal loans and contacted all my former business associates for the required funds to remodel, decorate and stock my new store -

## SCOTT NEWMAN JEWELERS!

It was very important to hire a topnotch sales staff so I immediately thought of Maria Alvarez, the dark haired Marilyn Monroe lookalike who had worked for me at Litton Jewelers. I called her store, but sadly she didn't work there anymore and left no forwarding phone number. So what the hell, I put an ad in the 'Personals' section of the local newspaper:

*'Maria formerly of Litton Jewelers. This is Scott. Call me ASAP. Contact the newspaper for my private #'*

Sure enough, a couple of days later she called. "Scott, it's Maria, how are you? I saw your ad and was curious why you were trying to get in touch with me."

"Maria, I'm opening my own jewelry store at a high end fashion square on the Upper East Side and would love for you to come work for me as the lead salesperson. You were the best at Litton Jewelers and I want the best for my store."

"Actually Scott, your timing is great. I can start anytime you'd like."

After I hired my sales staff, it was time to implement phase two of the Scott Newman Jewelers marketing and promotion plan.

71

Since I had already convinced Mr. Elias to lease me the store with no money down, then certainly I could convince the billboard companies and radio stations to front me advertising time as well.

The key to phase two was exploiting the local media to promote and publicize my campaign. Complete media saturation was my goal. Every resident of New York City would know about 'Christmas in July' at Scott Newman Jewelers. Commercials and promos would run on the top six radio stations. Billboards in key locations would feature Santa and his helpers. Moving billboards would cruise up and down major boulevards. And just to insure all the bases were covered, airplanes towing giant banners across the sky would dominate the New York skyline during the morning and evening commuter rush hours.

Riding my wave of optimism, my first stop was the top radio station with the largest listening audience in the city. I presented my ten day marketing plan to a sales representative, a sweet lady named Lana. "I have a large New York wholesaler who has agreed to place over a million dollars worth of beautiful jewelry in my store during this extraordinary promotion. I will offer the lowest prices in the country and my store will be open from eight in the morning until midnight every day of the ten day sale. All sales will be cash or credit cards. No layaways."

Lana viewed me with unveiled skepticism, but I didn't skip a beat.

"Lana, it's 'Christmas in July'! People will believe it when they see my store fully decorated and my sales force outfitted in festive Christmas costumes with Santa Claus greeting everyone at the door. The store will be so packed, a long line of anxious customers no doubt will be waiting for their turn to get the best deal anywhere on jewelry. No one has ever done a promotion like this before."

Suddenly Lana became very enthused with the idea and laid out an advertising schedule. "We can do this for twelve thousand dollars with fifty percent down," she proposed.

"Lana, I will be bringing in large amounts of cash each day. Come by the store after six p.m. and I will pay you cash for each day's advertising. If I don't have the money, you simply pull the rest of the ads. The worst case scenario for you is losing a single day's cost."

The light in her eyes quickly faded and she looked at me like I was from another planet. "There is no way my company would agree to this. No one does business like this."

"You're right Lana. No one does business like this, but like I said earlier, no one has ever done a promotion like this. Let me ask you a favor, Lana. Present this plan to your boss. See what he thinks. I'd really appreciate it."

She reluctantly agreed but two days later, Lana delivered the bad news. The boss wasn't interested. Unfazed, I contacted another radio station and pitched the same offer to a sales rep whose cold response echoed Lana's: 'no one does business like this'.

I didn't want to lose any more time by asking a favor so I simply requested that the sales rep set up an appointment with the general manager. She agreed but cautioned me that it would be a waste of my time. There was no way he would be interested.

The next day I found myself proposing my marketing plan not to the general manager but the president of the radio station! I delivered an Oscar winning performance that guaranteed the plan's success. I emphasized that 'Christmas in July' was a unique promotion no one had ever done before. I could see I was slowly convincing him and finally he nodded, shook my hand and agreed to take the chance.

The news of my advertising deal with no 'up front money' spread like wild fire and all the other advertisers fell in line. And so began 'Christmas in July'.

Call me crazy but I trusted my instincts. I knew this idea was a winner. I began by complementing the interior and exterior of the store with dazzling Christmas decorations. Red and green ribbons encircled the ceiling where sparkling styrofoam images of bells, stars and snowflakes were hung. The finishing touch was genuine mistletoe, lots and lots of mistletoe. There's nothing like a sweet Christmas kiss to celebrate the spirit of the holiday!

A beautifully decorated Christmas tree occupied one corner of the store and Christmas stockings dangled from the mantel of a faux fireplace in the opposite corner. The windows were fringed with frost and holly wreaths adorned the walls. Santa Claus greeted everyone with a candy cane as they entered the store. My sales staff was attired in Christmas costumes: the men dressed as Santa's elves and the ladies in lovely red Santa dresses trimmed with white fur. The Christmas atmosphere was highlighted with complimentary eggnog and hot chocolate for all my customers.

The ad campaign started four days before the big event and the highlight was the most popular radio Dee Jay in New York doing live spots on the air as well as some remote spots from the store throughout the ten day sale. I was psyched! All my hard work, diligent preparations and unwavering belief in myself was finally going to pay off. The store was perfectly decorated, the staff was buzzing with enthusiasm and the display cases were overflowing with gorgeous jewelry pieces.

On the first day of 'Christmas in July', we had a staff meeting at seven a.m. to prepare for the grand opening at eight a.m. Pulling into the fashion square parking lot, I couldn't believe my eyes because it was already half full! I knew those were my customers since the fashion square didn't officially open until nine. When Santa opened the door at precisely eight o'clock, he had to step back to avoid the crush of customers who had already been waiting in line for hours.

My staff always asked the customers what brought them into the store and the response was almost unanimous: they could not go anywhere in the city without being bombarded with 'Christmas in July' ads on every radio station, or plastered on billboards by the side of the road or moving billboards in traffic or the banners soaring overhead in the sky.

The store was packed to the rafters every day. There was a constant flow of customers from opening to closing. It never let up. The ad campaign was so effective, I had customers traveling from distances of more than one hundred miles away. In fact, things got so crazy that I had to install a ticket machine at the entrance where Santa passed out numbers to the eager customers anxiously waiting outside.

Every day the various ad sales reps would show up at six p.m. for their ad payments and the store was always so busy even they had to wait. Mr. Elias occasionally stood outside and watched the sales pandemonium in disbelief. Seeing is believing. Rather than struggle through the crowd, he just phoned me his congratulations. I even got calls from former co-workers telling me they just saw one of my moving billboards passing by on the street. Some complained about the lack of traffic in their stores because several of their most loyal customers were buying jewelry at Scott Newman Jewelers.

Just like Mr. Elias and the advertisers, Amy was now a believer. "I will never doubt you again Scott. When you have an idea no matter how crazy it sounds, nothing stops you."

The ten day sale flew by and on the last day we were mobbed with customers from eight a.m. to midnight just like the first day. We didn't close until one in the morning after every customer had finally been accommodated.

I thanked the staff for their hard work and sent them home to enjoy a good night's sleep. I was so hyped up I knew it would be impossible to sleep so I just started cleaning up. Just as she had done from the very first day, Maria stayed behind and helped me straighten up the entire store. I was on such a high I didn't even know what time it was.

When we finished our chores, Maria turned to me and said, "Mr. Newman, I've never seen anything like this. This was the most exciting sales experience I have ever been a part of. Thank you for allowing me to share in it. You are truly a marketing genius."

"Think of it as a great team effort," I said. "You were fantastic and I owe you a thank you as well, and for chrissakes, would you stop calling me Mr. Newman."

"Okay, Mr. New ... Scott. Would you mind just moving over here for a sec." She took my arm and guided me a couple of steps forward. "There we go, that's perfect. Now look up and tell me what you see."

"Mistletoe. Lots and lots of mistletoe."

"Right you are. Do you know what two people are supposed to do when they are standing under lots and lots of mistletoe, you know, to celebrate the spirit of Christmas?"

She didn't wait for an answer and cupped my neck with her hand and softly kissed my lips. I felt the touch of her other hand on my neck as her kiss grew stronger and longer as she guided me gently into Santa's sleigh. And yes, I believe the spirit of Christmas is an experience that everyone should enjoy.

When the sale was over and all my expenses were paid, I ended up with a net profit of more than one hundred thousand dollars. Of course, business didn't continue booming like that, but due to the tremendous success of 'Christmas In July' and word of mouth, we had a steady flow of customers.

I had been working tirelessly without a break when the opportunity to fly to Los Angeles for a jewelry show came up and Amy didn't want to go. The stress from the 'Christmas in July' sale still lingered and I really needed to take a breather and relax a little.

I wondered if Heidi Palmer from my Lumina Pearl days was still in the Los Angeles area or perhaps somewhere in Europe modeling for some famous painter. Among her numerous talents, she had an amazing eye for jewelry. I tried everything I could think of to track her down but came up empty. So I took another shot in the dark and placed an ad in the 'Personals' section of the Los Angeles Times newspaper:

*'Heidi Palmer. Formerly of Lumina Pearls. Call Scott from same. Contact the paper for my private #'*

She responded the day after the ad was published.

She was not at all surprised to hear about my successful 'Christmas in July' sales event and very eager to join me in exploring the exciting spectacle of the world's finest jewelry collections and displays. I needed her discerning eye for elegance

78

to confirm my selections that would highlight my next 'Christmas in July' event. We went out to dinner every evening and on one occasion I insisted that we experience the magnificent view from the top of the Hollywood Holiday Inn revolving restaurant.

I reserved the same table that Dennis Milton and Brad Goodman were cozied up with their respective companions, the 'average' housewife from the Lumina promo film and the hot Lumina receptionist. Once the wine was poured, I related the story of unmasking those two hypocrites and eventually resigning from the organization by smashing my company Cadillac into the wall next to the Lumina Board Room picture window. She laughed so hard I thought she might choke on her wine. When she caught her breath, she added that both of those scumbags had propositioned her so many times she lost count.

When I asked her what she was doing now that the Lumina pyramid had collapsed, she just gave me one of her enigmatic smiles and said she was keeping busy. I wondered how an intriguing 'free spirit' like Heidi stays 'busy'. I recalled the exotic nude paintings at the villa and how I suspected that she was actually the model.

We were intensely 'busy' during the nights we shared in the hotel until the jewelry show was over. Although we agreed to stay in touch, I figured the next time I saw her would be in an art gallery where she would be surrounded by art lovers admiring her enchanting painted image.

Back in New York, Bob Rosen dropped by the store. He was a good customer of mine, always friendly and polite. One day he mentioned that he and his partner owned a telemarketing company selling maintenance supplies and light bulbs to large multi-million dollar companies located all over the country. He revealed matter of factly that both of them were making well over a quarter of a million dollars a year in commissions.

"You're a natural salesman, Scott. People love you. I have no doubt that you would be great in this business. You've been blessed with a winning personality and I know you could easily make the money that I'm making. Take my card and if you're interested, give me a call."

I thanked Bob and told him how much I appreciated it, but I was happy and doing well in the jewelry business. Little did I know that my jewelry business prosperity was about to evaporate.

In October, I began planning another spectacular sales event and this time it would actually occur during the Christmas season. I was confident this event would easily eclipse the previous 'Christmas in July' sale if I simply duplicated the same successful marketing strategy. However, most of the ad reps advised me against spending so much money because the previous 'Christmas in July' event had already developed a customer base that normally would take an average business years to establish. They assured me that all my existing customers would be returning anyway.

Unfortunately, I did not heed these words of wisdom and forged ahead with the same advertising blitz using the same media. I worked out a deal with all my advertisers to pay ten per cent up front and then the balance at the end of the sales period.

The sale kicked off fifteen days before Christmas and this time we were open twenty four hours a day, nonstop for fifteen days. The sales staff and Santa were all geared up for the incredible sales bonanza, but when the door opened for business, Santa stood there almost alone. The long line of anxious customers did not materialize. Stragglers and window shoppers wandered in occasionally, but they were just part of the usual fashion square traffic. Where were the regular customers? The answer, as I sadly discovered, was that everyone had purchased their Christmas gifts during the July sale when the prices were so incredibly low.

As the days of the sale passed, my optimism never wavered, but my store remained pretty much a ghost town. Reality hit home when we closed up on the last day of the event. The sale had been a total disaster. There would be no Maria under lots and lots of mistletoe. I owed money left, right and center including over one hundred thousand dollars to the advertisers. I had no choice. I had to declare bankruptcy.

My dreams were shattered. Scott Newman Jewelers was history. The New Year for me wasn't very happy. I had no idea what I was going to do. Rather than mope around in my house, I went outside every day for a long run through the park to clear my mind. Suddenly a light went on in my head.

Bob Rosen and the telemarketing business! I raced back home. Luckily, I still had his card and gave him a call. I told him straight up about the jewelry store disaster and that I was looking to open a new chapter in my life.

"You may not believe me now Scott, but your 'disaster' may turn out to be the best thing that ever happened to you!"

# Chapter Five

## LIGHTBULBS TO GOLD

I was pumped with optimism as I entered the restaurant to meet with Bob Rosen. I knew in my gut this was a perfect opportunity for me. No time to waste. Let's get this show on the road! Bob was waiting for me at a table tucked away in the back of the restaurant where we had complete privacy.

I thanked Bob for meeting with me.

"Don't give it a second thought Scott," he said. "I know talent when I see it and you, my friend, have it in spades." I listened carefully as he explained in great detail how the industry worked. "Scott, with your dynamic personality and your smooth Dee Jay voice, you are a natural closer on the phone. You'll be a great 'bulber'. That's what we are called in our industry. Both my partner and I make over three hundred thousand dollars a year and I am positive that you will too."

"That's a lot of money Bob," I said with a bit of skepticism. "Most working folks don't even come close to making a six figure salary. Don't take this wrong, but are we talking about a legitimate business?"

"Of course, Scott," he chuckled. "No worries. The lightbulb business is just like any other business. You can charge any price you want as long as you don't misquote or intentionally deceive the customer by giving him a low price and then billing him later with a higher price."

"Okay," I said somewhat relieved. "I understand that you need to be honest with the buyer, but what kind of mark ups are you talking about?"

"We work on a ten to fifteen times markup ratio which is completely legal. For example, our cost for a four foot fluorescent tube is two dollars. We increase the price to twenty five dollars and that is the exact price we quote to the buyers. We don't lie to them and screw them later by billing them for a higher price per tube. Marking up prices is a business practice that is typical of most industries anywhere in the world."

"Alright Bob, I'm all in. When do I start? How about today?"

"Slow down a minute Scott," he chuckled. "First you have to be trained. My partner and I work together out of a small office. We don't have sales people. It's just the two of us and that's how we like it. So let me tell you exactly what I did to get into this business. Like I said, first you have to go through a training period of about three months. And the only company that hires people with no experience is Rusmark Products. Jack Nestor is the owner and he places a weekly ad in the newspaper for new salespeople with no experience.

This industry is full of paranoid owners. They don't trust anyone. They think everyone is out to steal accounts from them. Don't tell Nestor that you know me. You need to give him the impression that you don't know a thing about this industry. However," Bob continued with a smile and a wink. "As you already know, the key in any business is the 'sales pitch' and in our industry, mine is the best. And here's how it goes…"

I listened to Bob like he was sharing one of the great secrets of the universe and memorized every word. I wanted to nail this opportunity from the get go.

"Once you're trained," Bob continued, "your next step is getting a sales job with Prospect Lighting. It's a very successful company owned by a couple of Italian guys, Donny Ricci and Steve Moreno, and they only hire experienced salespeople with established accounts. That's the place where you're going to make a ton of money."

I thanked Bob for his advice and also for taking a great load off my mind. The second I left the restaurant I called Rusmark and made an appointment with the owner, Jack Nestor, for an interview the following day. I didn't sleep much that night, but I was riding high with enthusiasm when I entered his office. Nestor cut right to the chase and said that he was impressed with my confident and persuasive phone voice and offered me three hundred dollars a week to start. I told him honestly that I need six hundred dollars a week to cover my living expenses.

"Are you kidding me, everyone starts at three hundred dollars a week, take it or leave it," Nestor said with finality.

"No offense Mr. Nestor, but I'm not 'everyone'. Give me a chance to demonstrate what I can do for you. Give me a dead account and I'll show you that I can be the best salesman you ever had. I'm gonna make you a ton of money."

Nestor was losing his patience. "Hold on there, Mr. Newman. You have no experience in this business. Do you think you can just walk in here and re-sell a dead account that my best sales guys already gave up on and buried. That's why it's called a dead account. I think you're getting way too far ahead of yourself. Just take the three hundred dollars a week and pay your dues here like everyone else."

"Just give me a chance, Mr. Nestor. Let me sit down with your best sales guy for half an hour so I can learn the pitch." Nestor rolled his eyes. "I'm serious. What have you got to lose?" Nestor shook his head in disbelief. "Well Mr. Newman, you got a pair of balls, I'll give you that, but this is a complete waste of time, except for maybe a few laughs."

I spent some time with the guy Nestor assigned to tutor me and although I listened attentively, my confidence was sky high because I knew I was going to use the Bob Rosen pitch. When the short lesson was over, I asked for Mr. Nestor's permission to add a couple of things of my own to the pitch. Nestor just shrugged his shoulders and impatiently led the way to the salesroom jumping with activity. The chatter of dozens of enthusiastic guys on the phone dominated the room.

"Listen up fellas," Nestor announced and the room volume quickly lowered. "Anybody got a dead account from over a year ago? I'm talking about a graveyard dead account. Something that was really good for a while and then went to hell overnight."

One guy raised his hand thinking this was his chance to score some points with the boss. He dug through a pile of cards and proudly handed one over to Nestor who glanced at it and laughed. "Yeah, I remember this one," shaking his head. "It was worth about twenty to thirty thousand a month and the buyer was a great 'whale' for a couple of years and then it suddenly died. We tried to revive it with no luck at all and we never did find out why we lost it."

He held up the card for everyone to see. "Okay guys, this is Mr. Newman and he's going to perform mouth to mouth resuscitation on this cadaver!" They all roared with laughter as Nestor handed me the card and waited for the inevitable disaster to unfold.

"Mr. Nestor, I'd like to re-open this account at around ten thousand dollars, would that be okay?" Nestor just chuckled, put the phone on speaker and announced that it was 'show time'.

OK boys, 'watch and learn'. I dialed the number with great confidence because I was going to use Bob Rosen's pitch for the first time. The phone rang several times before a voice curtly said hello. "Hi Joe," I said enthusiastically. "I can't believe I finally got through to you. You're harder to reach than my wife's boyfriend." He laughed so I knew he was a good guy. "How ya doing buddy, this is Ron Harper, the owner over at Rusmark Products. Relax because I'm not calling you about an order. When the owner calls, it's gotta be good news, right Joe?

I'm calling to tell you how much I appreciate your business. I'm sending you thirty 'Benjamins'. That's three thousand dollars as a thank you. I am not going to waste your time sending chump change Visa or Home Depot cards. You're one of my good guys Joe and I always take care of my good guys. There's only one condition Joe. Don't forget me when something comes up okay? Is that fair enough? You got a pen handy? Here's your Priority Overnight tracking number - E 223 525 237 - repeat it back to me. You can track it after five p.m. today. I'm sending the thirty 'Benjamins' to your home address. You haven't moved on me have you Joe? Are you still at 2155 Solano Street in Dallas, Texas 78218? Great!

I gotta ask you a question Joe. Are you a married guy like me? Yeah? I bet you've been married for many years and I'm sure she's a great lady so promise me you'll take really good care of her OK? Listen Joe, not for now, it's for the end of the month. You're using four and eight foot florescent tubes and four and

88

eight foot ballasts, right? I know you use a lot of these so I'll keep it real small and put you down for three separate orders. One case of tubes and one case of ballasts on each order.

Don't worry. I'm the owner so I can invoice these orders two weeks apart so you don't get one large eight thousand dollar invoice like my dip shit salesman did to you before. Isn't that the reason why you stopped buying from us? Well guess what my friend, that will never happen again because I'm giving you my personal cell number. You will be dealing with me directly from now on. Save it in your phone. 212-555-0298, got it? Perfect.

Now write this down. Today is September 15. I'll date the first order with today's date for one case of four tubes and one case of four foot ballasts. I'll ship it tomorrow and the invoice will follow in about five days. I'll date the second order September 29 and the last order will be dated October 14, that way you won't be getting the merchandise in one day with one large bill. I'll keep each invoice at about thirty three hundred dollars and you'll have your thirty 'Benjamins' tomorrow. Fair enough?"

Joe enthusiastically expressed how much he appreciated me and how great it was doing business with me. "Ok Joe, just give me three purchase order numbers. I'll attach a different P.O. number to each order." Joe said that he left his purchase order book in the other office. With authority, I told Joe that I'll hold while he retrieves his book. When he came back on the line in less than a minute and gave me the P. O. numbers, I noticed the laughter in the sales room had ceased.

Rows of blank faces were staring at me in stunned silence. After Joe gave me the P. O. numbers I continued. "By the way Joe, my good guys always get their gifts first and I always make sure I take care of them for the holidays. Thanksgiving and Christmas are coming up so I'll be calling you a week before each holiday and I promise that you will enjoy all your holidays like never before. All right my friend, have a great day and when you get the thirty 'Benjamins' tomorrow, you'll remember who you're dealing with. Ron Harper. The 'Benjamin King' who always keeps his word!"

Most of the sales people were shaking their heads in amazement before settling back to work while Nestor and I returned to his office. I asked him about the cost of the goods on the order I just placed and he said around a thousand dollars. "Then the sale I just made was for ten thousand dollars with a sales commission of thirty five per cent less my portion of the gift. Right? So Mr. Nestor, my first commission check will be around twenty three hundred dollars. Is that correct?"

He nodded 'yes'. "And there won't be a problem with a six hundred dollar a week salary as a draw against commissions?" Nestor genuinely laughed and shook my hand and said that I would make a great addition to his organization.

I rushed home to tell Amy the great news about my new sales job with Rusmark. I told her that I made a two thousand dollar commission on the first day and I was starting at six hundred dollars a week. Once I was trained and had my own accounts, there was going to be some serious money coming in.

To my surprise, she tossed cold water all over it. "This is not a job. It's a scam. Why don't you look for a real job that has some security and includes health and retirement benefits?"

I was momentarily stunned by the negative response and patiently explained. "Amy it's not a scam. It's for real. I saw Bob's commission checks. He really does make over three hundred thousand dollars a year. What happened to my girl who said to me after the huge success of 'Christmas In July' that she would never doubt me again. Listen honey, I love you but let me explain something to you. First of all, I'm not looking for a dead end job with so called job security that pays a shit salary. I'm not going to work my ass off for the next twenty five or thirty years for some bullshit corporation that will eventually dismiss me with a gold watch and say 'enjoy your retirement' as I'm walking out the door.

Screw that. If you want a husband that would be happy with that kind of insignificant life style, then let's end our marriage right now and remain friends because here's the deal. I am going to become extremely rich with or without you. So decide right now if you want the same life style making tons of money, driving expensive cars, buying whatever we want and taking great vacations. That is where I am headed and I hope with all my heart that you want to be with me so what do you want to do Amy?"

She threw her arms around me and said, "Scott I love you so much. I am with you one hundred percent and I promise I will do my best to believe in your dreams too."

Dennis Harwell was assigned as my trainer. The very first thing he wanted me to do was listen to the other salesmen pitching companies over the phone. I was not surprised to hear them speaking to Maintenance Managers and Purchasing Agents for the first time as if they had been doing business together for years. And these were first time cold calls! Just like Bob Rosen had coached me on the sales pitch, their conversations were scripted and precise: "I really appreciate your business. We just finished a huge contract with the depot, you know, Home Depot. As a thank you for your business, I'm sending you a Home Depot card as a gift. Just enjoy it. Buy something really nice for yourself, you deserve it. Just don't forget me when something comes up OK?"

Then the pitch continued. "In order to insure that you receive your gift card safely, what's your home address?" At this point, if the guy doesn't give his home address, the salesman would hang up the phone and then dial up the next company. I asked Dennis why the salesmen were hanging up the phone when they were not getting the home address. He explained that these guys work for big companies and they buy their maintenance products from numerous suppliers so we're looking for that one guy who is already taking gifts from other maintenance suppliers. We call this customer a 'taker' or a 'mooch'. This is someone who could care less about the prices we are charging his company. He just wants something for himself and will happily give out his home address.

The pitch is all about selling the sizzle (gift), not the steak (product). So when you are pitching the gift, you really have to project excitement. You let him know it's a really nice size gift card. You encourage him to pick out something really nice because he really deserves it. Tell him that one of your customers just picked out a top of the line Weber barbecue grill. Then you get his home address."

Wait a minute Dennis, I reflected. If every company has the same 'gift' policy (Visa or Home Depot cards or maybe some petty cash like ten or twenty dollar bills) then the 'sizzle' is basically the same throughout the industry. What I need is a 'game changer' to separate myself from the rest of the pack and become the top 'bulber' in the industry. I recalled my successful sales performance for Jack Nestor. The key was the 'Benjamins'. That buyer didn't know me from Adam and gave me an order like we were best friends. I'll just keep this strategy to myself and wait until the time is right to introduce myself as the 'King of Benjamins'.

Dennis resumed the pitch with the dialogue lines and directions for the close of the sale. "I just kept it real small for now and left you with half a box of the four foot fluorescent tubes. That will give me a little something over here until I touch base with you in a few months. Fair enough? If he is still the right guy he'll say okay or that's fine. It's only a small order but I still appreciate it. Again, enjoy your gift. Oh, by the way, what purchase order number should I use this time?

This is the last step and will determine whether it's a done deal. If he's not a 'mooch', he'll say he really doesn't need anything at this time or he'll request prices. In a situation where the customer asks about prices, he's probably not a 'mooch'. I would simply give him our price and he would either give an order or say the price is too high. Either way, I would thank him for his order or tell him that if he changes his mind to please give me a call."

Dennis turned me loose and I hit the phones like a hungry lion and quickly began closing customers. This was great. It was like second nature to me. My confidence was growing on a daily basis as I developed some very nice accounts and at this point, my colleagues already viewed me as a real 'bulber'. The three month training period was suddenly over and my thoughts turned to Bob Rosen's next piece of career advice: Prospect Lighting.

Donny Ricci and Steve Moreno were the millionaire owners of Prospect. Steve did the hiring and determined the salaries while Donny was responsible for all the buying and managed the entire warehouse operation. When I called Prospect and spoke with Steve, I told him I worked for Jack Nestor at Rusmark Products and that I was looking to make a change. I assured him that I had experience and some really good accounts. That's all Steve needed to hear. He loved stealing sales people from Nestor because of their nasty history.

Steve and Donny had formed a small start-up company in the 1960's and over the years built it into a multi-million dollar lighting company. Jack Nestor was their top salesman as well as the General Manager. He was in charge of the entire salesforce and had access to all of the company's accounts. But Nestor had secretly formed his own company, Rusmark, and moved all of Prospect's accounts over to Rusmark before anyone could blink. With the stolen accounts, he became a millionaire almost overnight. It was the ultimate act of betrayal and Steve and Donny enjoyed nothing more than hiring Nestor's sales people.

During our initial phone conversation, Steve asked the usual interview questions including what high school I had attended. "Do you know Doug Kaufman?"

"Yes," I answered, "we graduated in the same class."

Steve continued enthusiastically. "Doug is one of my top salespeople and he's making over two hundred thousand dollars a year. I want you to know that I get great pleasure out of paying huge salaries. So come on by the office and I'll have Doug join us so you can hear from him about the wonderful opportunities here at Prospect."

When I pulled into the Prospect Lighting parking lot in my four year old Chevy sedan, I couldn't help but notice the BMW's, Porsches, and Mercedes parked everywhere except for this one orphan Dodge that was much older and in far worse shape than mine. Maybe it's a new guy like me. Then I saw Doug Kaufman emerge and lock the door. Must be a loaner. His Mercedes is probably in the shop. Little did I know…

The interview went well and I was thrilled. My starting salary was a thousand dollars a week. Steve said his expectations were very high for me and he was sure I had the talent and motivation to meet those goals. The meeting ended with his promise that we would talk again in ninety days about a higher salary. Amazing. A discussion about a raise without me asking first. Doug Kaufman would later confirm that Steve was the only owner in the industry who did not hesitate to pay large salaries.

Doug immediately took me under his wing and showed me the ropes. As my mentor, he taught me his surefire selling techniques, however, the sales leads that we were given were not very promising. They consisted of older, stale and recycled leads for companies that had been previously doled out to other sales people. The only other viable source for leads was cold calling potential customers out of the Manufacturers Directories which were universally available to anyone who wandered into a public library.

The immediate goal was to get the name of the maintenance manager or purchasing agent or any other authorized buyer in charge of ordering the lightbulbs and maintenance supplies. But this strategy was damn near impossible to achieve because the receptionists for these companies were stationed there to screen the flood of incoming phone calls from dozens of lighting and maintenance companies just like ours. Almost every receptionist was trained to ask a series of standard qualifying questions: 'What is the purpose of this call? What is your name? What is the name of your company?'

More than eighty per cent of the time they put you on hold and talked to the buyer who obviously doesn't recognize our company's name as we never did business with them. She usually responded with the standard bullshit brush-offs like he doesn't know you and he's not interested or he's in a meeting (bullshit) or leave your name and number and he'll call you back (never happens) or I'll connect you to his voicemail and he will return your call (which they never do). So we'd have to make hundreds of calls just to find a few receptionists who were willing to give us the buyer's name and actually connect us to him.

There had to be an easier way to achieve this and once again, I came up with a great idea. I knew that Steve wouldn't go for the extra expense so I convinced Doug that we should hire two women as 'front loaders'. All day long, the 'front loaders' made dozens of cold calls to obtain the names of the authorized buyers and this saved us an unbelievable amount of productive time. We paid them eight dollars an hour and a five dollar bonus for every home address they scored.

The largest wholesaler of maintenance supplies in the country was Universal Industrial Supply. Almost every company purchases some of their supplies from them. Universal also had the largest catalogue. The next part of my idea was the 'phone script' I created for our two 'front loaders'.

"Good morning. This is Debbie from Universal Industrial Supply, we're one of your vendors. We just published our new maintenance catalogue and we're sending it out to all our customers. Whose attention should I direct the new catalog to?" After getting the name she asks for his title. "Is he authorized to order the maintenance supplies? Okay great, thanks. Now we also have a new warehouse catalogue. Do you have a warehouse manager who is authorized to purchase warehouse supplies? Thank you. You are very helpful, I appreciate your time. Just two more questions if you don't mind. Many of our customers have plant managers and operation managers who are authorized to order the maintenance supplies. Do you have a plant or operation manager who is authorized to do so? And of course, we always send the catalogue to the purchasing agent. Great, thank you for your time and have a great day."

My innovative strategy was a complete winner. Our 'front loaders' were doing extremely well collecting the names of authorized buyers from all over the country. When Doug and I made our calls, we simply asked the receptionist to connect us to a specific individual in the maintenance department for example. Nine out of ten times she would do so without screening the call. The results were amazing. Now that we had direct access, we were able to speak to more buyers in a day than a week or two of cold calls.

I had the 'front loaders' making similar calls as well. They would delay their calls for two days after receiving a buyer's name and then read from another 'phone script' that I had thoroughly prepared. "Good morning. Greg in maintenance please." Again, the receptionist would usually put the call right through.

"Good morning Greg. It's Debbie over with the maintenance supplies. You're a tough guy to reach, they should be paying you two salaries." If he was any kind of good guy that we could potentially sell, then he would laugh. "I'm not calling you about an order, relax. I have some good news for you. Something special just came up here. We finished a huge contract with Visa and they sent over a whole bunch of their Visa gift cards, you know the ones that are valid anywhere.

The owners of our company are sending them out to all the accounts. It's a thank you for your business because we certainly appreciate it. There is no charge, just enjoy it. The cards are being sent out by Two Day Priority Mail so I just need to fill out your card for you. Spell your last name for me and give me the home address again to make sure you get it safely."

If the guy is interested and wants the gift he will give his home address. If he declines and gives the company address then ninety nine per cent of the time he cannot be sold. At that point, I instructed the women to hang up and make their next call.

However, if the guy does give out his home address, then he is almost certainly a 'mooch' and she continues. "Great Greg, enjoy your gift card and one more thing. Scott, the head guy who sends out the gift cards will call you shortly to go over your home address and give you the Priority Mail tracking number so you can track your envelope. To make sure he connects with you quickly so he can send out your gift today, what's your cell number? Thank you, Greg. It was nice talking with you, enjoy your gift card and have a great day."

The next step was my follow up phone call. "Hey Greg, it's Scott over at the warehouse. I just got a fax from Debbie regarding your Visa gift card. Debbie's handwriting is terrible, she writes like a doctor so I want to make sure I am sending your Visa card to the correct address. Listen Greg, I'm sending your gift card by Priority Mail and you'll have it in two days. Let me give you the tracking number so you can track your envelope. Do you have a pen handy?" I give him the number and tell him he can track it later in the afternoon.

With an opening order, we send a fifty dollar Visa gift card and at this point he has no idea about the value of the gift card so I continue. "Greg, I really appreciate your business so with our really good guys, I'm putting an extra gift card in your envelope. These are not ten or fifteen dollar cards, they are real nice size gift cards, just don't forget me when something comes up OK?"

They will always say 'no problem' so if I get the sale I will put two twenty five dollar Visa cards in his envelope with a beautiful Thank You Card. When he receives it he'll remember me and there is a very good chance that he will make sure his company pays our invoice. There is an equally good chance to re-sell him again since he knows that when I tell him he's getting a gift, he knows that it will happen.

"Listen Greg, our salesman won't be out in your area to service your account for a couple of months so I kept it real small for later this month. I left you at just a half box of the four foot florescent tubes, that'll give me a little something over here. You'll have your gift card in two days, fair enough?" The right guy should say okay or 'no problem'. "Thank you, I really appreciate the small order and again enjoy your gift cards and oh I almost forgot. What Purchase Order number should I use this time?" After I get the PO number, I tell him to make a note that the lights are coming in from the factory over at Prospect, and of course, have a great day.

Our sales numbers increased dramatically. Doug and I continued to make calls to buyers while the women worked the gift card strategy and we were each making five sales a day or about twenty five sales a week which was pretty damn good.

The first few months at Prospect passed by quickly. I was determined to climb to the top of the mountain and become the number one salesman. As I worked my butt to the bone, my thoughts were on another Prospect salesman, John Hartley. Out of nowhere, he zoomed ahead of the pack. He was selling tons of accounts and finding great leads like it was a walk in the park. On any given day, he would average selling ten to twelve accounts and for one salesman that was unheard of. It was crazy. He was selling just about every guy he called. Where could he be getting these great 'leads'? Come hell or high water, I was determined to find out how he was pulling this off without breaking a sweat.

101

One day I offered to buy him a beer after work and it turned out that we actually had a lot in common. He laughed his ass off when I told him the 'personal ad' stories of Maria Alvarez and Heidi Palmer. We started hanging out a bit and eventually became good friends. One evening after a couple of beers, I just came out and asked him how the heck he was getting those terrific 'leads' while I was sweating under a hot sun making dozens of cold calls all day long. He laughed and said that for the past couple of months he was dying to tell someone what he was up to, but there was no one he could really trust at Prospect.

"You're a good man Scott. You have that magic touch on the phone which is a very rare thing and you're the kind of guy that I would like to see have great success. I know I can share this with you and it will stay between us, but I want you to know that what I'm about to tell you will blow your mind and blast your sales into the stratosphere."

"Okay John," I exclaimed. "I'm all ears."

"The first thing you need to know is that what I'm getting are not 'leads'."

# Chapter Six

## FROM SHREDS TO RICHES

"These are not 'leads'. These are current ACCOUNTS," John declared with a straight face.

I was absolutely stunned. "What do you mean they're not 'leads'? You sell just about everyone you call." John assured me that these were bona fide accounts that really existed. The calls he was making were simply to sell them again. These were not 'cold calls' or follow up calls intended to convince someone to buy. These were buyers.

"This doesn't make any sense." I was completely perplexed. "How can you call real accounts? Do they just fall out of the sky? What am I missing here?"

"Let me explain," John continued. "We're sitting in the hub of the telemarking lightbulb business right? Many of these companies are located here in New York and North Jersey. Monday is the big day when all these companies receive checks from their customers who actually pay their invoices. These are called 'paid ups' and are extremely valuable because any company that paid a greatly inflated invoice will be easy to sell the next time around.

Here's the beauty of it Scott. These are actual paid up invoices, not 'leads' like the recycled 'leads' that Steve is handing out to all his sales people. I'm calling current accounts. Doug Kaufman does well because he usually works ten to twelve hours a day. He's on the phone from eight a.m. to five p.m. East Coast Time. Then another three hours to California making cold calls from the Manufacturers Directories. The guy eats lunch and dinner at his desk and never takes a break. Screw that.

What I have are real accounts. And they don't fall from the sky. They exist right here on earth in locations that no one would ever imagine. And they are procured through a very methodical procedure called 'trashing'."

"Trashing?" I said with great skepticism and confusion.

"Yes 'trashing'," John confirmed with a smile. Every Monday night after eleven p.m. when I'm sure that no one is around, I go 'trashing'. I basically go through the trash dumpsters of various lightbulb companies and remove the trash bags."

Now I was even more confused. "Why on earth would you be stealing garbage?"

His answer shocked me.

"What you call garbage Scott, I call money in the bank."

I still did not understand.

"The trash bags are full of papers that I carefully sift through. And what I find is a gold mine of paid up account invoices, check copies, the names and home addresses of the maintenance managers or purchasing agents and even the amounts of the gifts they receive!"

"That is unbelievable," I exclaimed. "Those papers give you direct access to buyers. No more bullshit cold calls, 'leads' or watch dog receptionists!"

"And here's the best part," John continued. "When I re-sell these paid up accounts, I either call the 'mooch' directly or request him by name to the receptionist who simply connects me. I say good morning, it's Joe from Prospect Lighting and pitch him the gift, then close him. It's all about the 'mooches' getting their piece of the action. They could care less about the name of the company or the inflated invoice."

John broke into laughter. "Scott, you're gonna love this story. I remember these two accounts of yours that I got out of the trash when you were still with Rusmark. When I first contacted the buyers, they said they were already buying from a guy named Scott at Rusmark. No problem, I assured them. I'm calling from Rusmark's parent company, Prospect. I'll be taking care of you

105

from now on with much better service and gifts. And please do not mention this to Scott the next time he calls for an order." John was laughing so hard he had to stop and catch his breath.

"Wait a second," I recalled. "They did tell me about a guy from Prospect taking over the accounts. That sly dog was you? You stole my accounts out of Rusmark's dumpsters?" John just nodded his head and we both started laughing hysterically. "You son of a gun, John. Man did you ever pull one over on me. But I gotta tell you my friend, this brilliant scheme of yours is so far under the radar that no one would ever dream this in a million years.

"Like I said before Scott, you're a good man, the kind of guy that I would like to see have great success. This will change your life and make you a great 'bulber', maybe even put you on 'easy street'. I want you to be my partner in my 'trashing' scheme. We'll bring the bags back to my apartment and split them up fifty - fifty. There are so many 'paid ups' that I could never call all of them by myself. I'm happy to share the riches."

And so began my 'trashing' adventures. Every Monday night, John and I would hit four or five dumpsters, especially Rusmark's, then return to his apartment, dump the paper contents on the floor and divide the treasures. Some of the bags contained only shredded documents that John dismissed as useless. He simply crossed them off his list of companies and didn't waste any more time on their dumpsters.

After the first month of 'trashing' had massively increased my sales, Doug Kaufman's curiosity got the best of him. Without revealing my 'trashing' scheme or jeopardizing my relationship with John, I offered Doug half of my new accounts in exchange for half of the commissions he generated. Doug was thrilled and so was I because I was making even more money.

One night as I was tossing another 'useless' trash bag of shredded docs back into John's apartment dumpster, I paused in mid heave and wondered how much gold I might be throwing away. Those shreds could be worth hundreds of thousands of dollars if not millions. My car was parked a couple spaces away so what the hell, let's give this a shot. I popped open my trunk and tossed the trash bag of shreds inside.

It was three a.m. when I carefully opened the bag of shreds onto the quilt covering my apartment floor. This was going to be a very tedious chore piecing all these small strips of paper together. Check this out Humpty Dumpty, I'm gonna put these scraps back together again no matter what. It was just like working on a puzzle. Patiently and meticulously, piece by piece, I reassembled the shreds.

After several cups of coffee, the early morning sun peaked through my window and I paused for a moment to review my progress. I had successfully recreated twelve documents. I exhaled a soft whistle of astonishment. I looked through the 'paid ups' from some of the biggest corporations in the country. I gazed at my handiwork in amazement and realized that I had just accomplished the first giant step forward 'From Shreds To Riches'!

I did not share this discovery with John. In fact, he loved my idea of opening the bags first to save time by simply leaving the trash bags with shreds in the company dumpsters. After the usual routine of splitting the invoices in John's apartment, I would say good night and circle back to the dumpsters containing the shreds and load up my car.

Out of the blue one day, John told me that he was retiring from our 'trashing' ventures and from Prospect as well. He shared his plan to move to California, buy a house on the beach and enjoy some of the prime years of his life. "I made a fortune Scott and I'm handing the baton to you because I know you want the same things." I wished John the best and watched my mentor and benefactor ride off into the sunset. Doug was the logical choice to become my 'trashing' partner.

My workload was becoming more intense but also more lucrative. The two 'front load' women working for Doug and I were providing great leads. There were the commission splits with Doug from the 'trashing' invoices and of course, my own new accounts from my shredding enterprise. It was ridiculous how many accounts we were selling each day. We had doubled the daily number of accounts we sold from six or seven to twelve or thirteen each and we were no longer wasting our time with Steve's shitty 'leads'. I did the math and even though Doug and I were hauling in great commission checks, Steve and Donny were getting filthy rich from our hard work.

Maybe we should think about working for ourselves.

Doug was making four thousand dollars a week and I was pulling down three thousand. He was thrilled with the money. I was not. We were bringing in roughly seventy thousand dollars a week in 'paid ups' which was completely unheard of for only two salesmen within our industry. We were under appreciated by Donny and Steve and most definitely under paid. It was time to ask for a raise. Doug almost passed out when I asked him to join me in Steve's office to request that he increase our weekly draws to six thousand dollars.

He was trembling with fear as he retreated to the safety of his office where he could hide out and weather the shit storm that he believed was coming. "You're on your own Scott. Don't mention my name. I want nothing to do with your crazy suicide mission. It was nice knowing you."

Okay Doug, tell me how you really feel. His chicken shit attitude actually reinforced my determination to get a raise. I summoned up my 'Incredible Hulk' attitude as I marched with purpose to Steve's office. This guy was making boatloads of dough and the proof was all around me. Steve's office reeked of money. He sat behind his huge oak desk surrounded by tuck and roll leather chairs. Several abstract paintings hung from the paneled walls. He was wearing a custom tailored suit that I'm sure cost more than my weekly salary. His trademark was an unlit Cuban cigar that always hung from his mouth. He leaned back in his captain's chair and motioned me to have a seat. Steve specialized in sign language and grunts because he rarely unclenched the cigar from his teeth. He looked at me and waited for me to begin the conversation.

"As you know Steve, I really enjoy working for you and I love my job. Now I don't want to seem greedy or ungrateful, but Doug and I are bringing in an average of seventy thousand dollars a week in receivables and I'm only making three thousand a week out of that very large number."

Steve grunted and for once took the cigar out of his mouth. "Don't get me wrong, Scott. I appreciate everything you and Doug have done for my company, but haven't we been more than fair with you? There are very few 'bulbers' in this industry worthy of that title AND making this kind of money. You're at the very top of the pay scale. But I understand where you are coming from. How about another five hundred dollars a week?"

He stood up and extended his hand to conclude the deal. I didn't move. He stared at me for a few seconds and sat back down. He wasn't happy and demanded to know what the hell was wrong with me.

I stared right back at him and stood my ground. "Name me two other people in this industry who are bringing in seventy thousand dollars a week." Silence. "That's what I thought. You and I both know that I could go out on my own, hire a collector for four hundred a week, a secretary to handle invoices and answer the phones, use my own wholesaler (like Buddy Foreman) who will deliver product to me and find a shipper for six hundred a week. The way I figure it, after I pay all the expenses (office, phone, rent, etc) I could make an easy fifteen thousand dollars a week. And don't forget that all our leads are 'paid up' accounts from your competitors.

Now imagine me and Doug as competitors. I really don't want the aggravation and bullshit that goes with running my own company, but that's one hell of a lot of money. Let's get serious Steve."

Steve eyed me again, clamped down on his cigar and asked me what I had in mind. I told him the solution was simple and fair. Just give me a three thousand dollar a week raise and I'll get back to making him shitloads of money.

Steve's cigar was too fat to swallow, but he certainly choked on it. "Are you out of your mind? I've never given a raise that big."

"And you've never had a salesman like me either. And you're right. I might be crazy, but the facts speak for themselves. With the revenue I generate for your company, you know damn well that I'm worth a hell of a lot more than six thousand dollars a week."

Steve placed his cigar in an empty ashtray, rose from his chair and studied the abstract painting on the wall behind him like there

111

was an answer in that incomprehensible orgy of colors and patterns that was so often passed off as 'art'.

Turning back to me he said, "Scott, I never thought I would say this, but I'd rather have you working for me than against me as a competitor."

This time I gladly accepted his handshake and gave him a big fat European kiss on each cheek. "That's why I love working for you Steve."

I returned to my office on cloud nine. There was a weak tap on my door and Doug peeked in expecting me to be packing up all my office stuff. His face registered his surprise and he asked what happened with Steve. I leaned back in my chair and just gave him a satisfied wink.

He bounded down the hallway like a jack rabbit on speed and within three seconds he was in Steve's office to confirm the new raise that he was too afraid to ask for himself. Doug and I continued to work relentlessly 'trashing' and accumulating more accounts than we could ever keep up with. The revenue we generated for Steve and Donny exploded as we added more and more accounts.

We had achieved 'superstar bulber' status in the industry, but you'd never know it judging by Doug's 'lifestyle'. He was still driving that embarrassing piece of shit Dodge. It was not a loaner like I assumed months ago when I first interviewed at Prospect. It was his preferred mode of transportation. And his poor wife drove a similar bucket of bolts too. But I still had to listen to him almost every damn day when he dreamed out loud about owning a brand new Mercedes.

"Hey Doug," I called him on it one day. "I know you love to save money like a chipmunk storing chestnuts for the long winter, but I gotta tell you as a friend, you're a penny-pinching cheapskate. You're making ridiculous money. I refuse to be a friend and partner to a guy who earns three hundred thousand a year and still drives that same broken-down Dodge. Come along with me to the Mercedes dealership this Saturday. The new models just arrived and I'm trading in my SL 500 for the new edition. And don't ask me for a discount on my 'trade in' because you're going to get yourself a new one too and then I won't have to listen to your fantasies anymore."

Oh no, not Doug. He planned to squeeze every last mile out of that decrepit Dodge and then buy another bargain basement junk heap to replace it. This guy made Scrooge look like a shopaholic.

I never paid much attention to the office gossip, but Doug had a reputation as a money grubbing tightwad who actually did horde his money like Scrooge. Doug's idea of a lunch break was going to the bank and fondling the cash in his safe deposit box. Rumor had it that he was closing in on half a million in cash and two million in stocks.

Enough was enough. I invited him and Sheila (his wife) to a Saturday Brunch at the Grand Hyatt hotel which just happened to be located across from the Mercedes dealership.

After lunch, we dragged Doug to the dealership. I tried to cheer him up, but he had the mournful look of a pall bearer carrying the coffin of his best friend. Sheila pulled me aside and asked me to do something to lighten his mood because she was afraid to get her hopes up.

"Trust me Sheila," I assured her. "He'll be so shocked when he sees me holding the keys to my new Mercedes SL 550 that he will match me because there's no way he's gonna let me be the only good guy."

It wasn't quite that easy. He disappeared, but I soon found him outside in the used car section standing next to a second hand SL 500. "Look at this beauty Scott," Doug expressed with excitement. "It's only five years old with 45,000 miles on the odometer and I can save at least twenty grand on this baby!"

"Come on Doug, you know you're being a complete jerk here. Get your ass into the showroom and pick out one of those magnificent new SL 500's. For once in your life stop pinching your pennies. You know we're going to be multi millionaires in the next couple of years so just do it."

He bought the white one because I already had the red one.

Amy's and my wedding anniversary was coming up and I remembered that she had her eye on a beautiful white convertible four seater E 350 when we were at the Mercedes dealership. I thought about how lucky I was to have such a wonderful wife who had remained loyally by my side in spite of all the shit she'd gone through with me.

I parked it in the driveway of our home, wrapped a big red bow around the hood of the car and called her on the phone and told her to come outside for a minute. She walked up to the car, touched the red bow and turned to me with a confused look on her face. I handed her the keys and said, "Babe it's all yours. Happy Anniversary!" She broke down in a hysterical flood of tears and threw her arms around me. A lot of guys forget their anniversary, but not me. It's a great feeling when you give your wife some happiness.

Later that week, we picked up Doug and Sheila for dinner in Amy's new Mercedes. When Doug saw what Amy was driving, his face went whiter than the white color of her car. I thought he was going to have a massive heart attack right there on his front lawn. He was pretty quiet throughout the dinner but I could hear the wheels turning in his head as he calculated the financial hit on his enormous stash. The next day, Sheila rolled up in front of our house in a brand new white E 350 Mercedes, the identical twin of Amy's.

It was no longer an industry secret that Doug and I were the undisputed number one telemarketing 'bulbers'. No one was remotely close to making our unbelievable salaries of six thousand dollars a week. Out of the blue came a call from Supreme Lighting. I was aware of Supreme and especially the feisty owner Sam Ross. He was known and feared throughout the industry for his reputation as a cutthroat, dog-eat-dog business man. His

115

General Manager, Jay Cohen, opened the phone call with a flood of compliments and congratulations for my remarkable sales record. He invited Doug and I to lunch and a tour of their operation.

I was reluctant at first because there was no way they could exceed or even match our current salaries so I declined the offer. Jay persisted and pointed out that Supreme was one of the largest companies in the tri-state area with more than forty telemarketers. He assured me that I had nothing to lose and guaranteed I would be surprised.

Surprised? Me? The surprise is coming your way pal when you discover that you are losing a shit load of accounts and have no idea why. I accepted the invitation.

The huge number of cars in Supreme's parking lot confirmed they were indeed a large company. Cohen met us in the lobby and we were quickly escorted to Sam Ross's office.

Mr. Ross did not possess an ounce of diplomacy and got right to the point. "Boys, I didn't ask you here to screw around. I'll start you guys at four hundred thousand dollars a year plus bonuses and incentives. Wrap up your shit at Prospect and I'll see you here the day after tomorrow."

Sam reminded me a lot of Sid, the asshole General Manager of the jewelry store I worked in as a kid. I was expecting him to throw a roll of paper towels at me and start screaming about the fingerprints on the glass cover of his desk. He glanced at his watch and stared us down impatiently waiting for an answer. "I am wealthy beyond anything you can imagine and no one else in this industry could even think about matching what I'm going to pay you guys."

I stared back at that arrogant bastard and was already one step ahead of his shady bullshit. That sneaky son of a bitch does not want Doug and me. He just wants our accounts. Okay Sam, two can play at this game. You'll never touch our accounts, but I already made it my mission to get my hands on yours. And you'll never know where that kick in the nuts came from. I glanced at Doug who was frozen to his chair and thanked Mr. Ross for his generous offer, however, it was a big decision. Give us a couple days to talk it over with our wives.

Doug couldn't wait to get the hell out of there, but I told him to hold on while I scoped out Supreme's dumpsters. We circled the parking lot and found them enclosed by an eight foot high chain link fence, securely chained and locked. "That's the end of that," Doug conceded. "We'll never get those accounts."

"Are you kidding me Doug," I laughed out loud. "You oughta know me by now. Do you think that goddamn fence is gonna stop me? I'll be hopping over it like a gazelle every Monday night."

Supreme was a stand alone company so the dumpsters contained only their trash. If I just grabbed their bags and left an empty dumpster it would eventually raise suspicions. The solution was easy. I purchased the identical trash bags Supreme used and filled them up with worthless paper and made an even exchange of the bags I removed. The next Monday night we did a trial run and it worked flawlessly. In the following weeks, we sold well over two hundred of Supreme's accounts. Thanks, Sam.

But Sam became suspicious when several of his salesmen complained that customers were not placing orders with Supreme because they had already purchased from Prospect Lighting. Sam knew this could not be a coincidence. It was not possible for Prospect to achieve this with simple 'cold calling'. He didn't know how we were doing it but he was positive we were stealing his accounts. Sam went on the war path. His wholesaler shipped directly to Supreme's warehouse and had no access to the accounts so that was a dead end. Sam would never think in a million years that someone was stealing his trash. It wasn't possible. Every document had been shredded into useless pieces of paper scraps and safely locked behind an eight foot fence.

Regardless of how it was happening, Sam knew without a doubt or a *shred* of evidence, exactly who was screwing him. Living up to his asshole reputation, he phoned Steve and immediately started screaming that Scott and Doug had stolen his accounts and therefore his precious money. "There's enough here for all of us to make a living. I never thought you would lower yourself to stealing accounts from your competitors. You are no better than those two scum bags who belong in prison."

Steve had absolutely no clue what Sam's lunatic rant was about, but he fired right back.

"Who the hell do you think you're talking to? We run a clean operation here. What proof do you have that we are stealing your accounts?"

"I'll prove it to you," Sam continued screaming. "You let me talk to those two fucking thieves face to face in your office with you and Donny there and they will confess like a couple of school boys."

Steve agreed to a meeting for later that afternoon and in the meantime called me and Doug into his office for our own little meeting. He was still pissed off when he motioned us to our seats with a wave of his huge unlit cigar. "I just got off the phone with that psychopath Sam Ross over at Supreme and he accused us, or should I say you two, of stealing dozens of his accounts. I don't give a damn about that lunatic. I just want to know what the hell is going on so I can handle the situation."

"I find that accusation very interesting Steve," I said evenly. "Did Sam happen to mention that recently we were invited to his office for a meeting? Did he mention that he offered us four hundred thousand dollars a year plus bonuses and incentives to leave Prospect?"

Steve yanked the cigar out of his mouth. His eyes were on fire. "You gotta be kidding. That conniving son of a bitch," he shouted.

"That's right," I continued. "That generous offer obviously meant taking our accounts with us. So who's the thief now? The only reason Doug and I took the meeting was to scope out their operation. We had no intention of leaving Prospect. We are way

119

too happy here. Yes, it's true that we are selling a ton of their accounts but we have no obligation to reveal our sources."

Steve finally cracked a smile. "The hell with Sam Ross. I don't give a rat's ass how you're getting his accounts. Just sell as many as you can get your hands on. By the way, Sam was going to be here this afternoon to confront you guys, but there's no need for a showdown now."

"No wait Steve," I interrupted. "Don't cancel the meeting. I want to watch that douchebag eat shit."

Doug breathed a huge sigh of relief. He wouldn't have to attend the 'meeting' or hide under his desk all afternoon.

Steve and I were already seated when Sam Ross stomped into Steve's office. He ignored my extended hand and my greeting as I cheerfully said it was so nice to see him again.

Steve took his cue perfectly. "Oh, you two know each other?"

Sam glared at me. "Sure thing Steve. Sam and I go way back," I said innocently.

"Cut the shit", Sam raged. "I want Mr. Newman to admit he's been stealing my accounts."

"Are you calling me a thief," I said coolly.

"Goddam right I am," he raged.

"Do you have any proof or are you just firing this bullshit out of your ass?"

"The proof is the fact you're selling dozens of my accounts and I haven't figured out how the hell you're doing it yet."

"It's called hard work Sam. Doug and I make hundreds of cold calls and you know damn well that the 'mooches' buy from more than one company so the odds are very good that we will probably sell a few of your accounts."

"Do you really think I'm some kind of idiot to swallow that? It's not just a few accounts. It's hundreds and the improbable Vegas odds on that happening is proof you're stealing my accounts."

"Speaking of theft Sam," Steve smoothly interjected. "I understand you tried to steal Mr. Newman and Mr. Kaufman away from Prospect with an outrageous offer you were sure they would never refuse."

"That was just business," Sam exploded.

"You're right Sam," Steve admitted. "Business is business and that's why we're going to continue to sell the hell out of your accounts. Now get the fuck out of my office."

I held the door open for Sam as he stormed out. "Enjoy the rest of your day asshole.

Three hundred thousand dollars a month was the latest number that Doug and I were generating for Prospect. I was beginning to sorely regret my decision to ask for six thousand a week. It should have been a hell of a lot more. Steve and Donny were making insane profits from the accounts we brought in and not from the shitty 'leads' they gave us. All they did was ship the merchandise.

This was a bad joke. I showed Doug some very basic arithmetic. We were making peanuts and we should be getting rich.

Why don't we start our own company and keep all that hard earned money for ourselves?

# Chapter Seven

# THE KEY TO THE GOLD

"No way," Doug cried in his usual state of hysteria whenever I came up with a bold and ingenious plan to advance our careers. "I'm making six thousand dollars a week. There's no way in hell I'm walking away from that kind of money."

It would have been easier to haul the Statue of Liberty on my back all the way across the country and drop it in the San Francisco Bay than to convince Doug to leave Prospect. So what to do with an immovable object named Doug. My trusty lightbulb lit up again with another great idea. We will form our own independent company while continuing to work at Prospect and call it Argon Industries.

There was only one small detail. Doug was not aware of the creation of Argon Industries until I showed him the New Jersey incorporation papers. New Jersey does not publish the names of incorporated companies or the officers. Doug figured that if he wasn't on board from the beginning then I would just forget about it. He figured wrong. Once he stopped whining and complaining, I shared my plan.

Instead of opening all our new accounts with Prospect, we will discretely open a few cream of the crop accounts with Argon. The profits from the Argon accounts will belong to us and not Donny and Steve. And those profits will make our six thousand dollar weekly salaries look like pocket change. The appeal of adding extra cash to his safe deposit box was more than Doug could resist.

As a firm believer in the 'law of attraction', I was not surprised when Buddy Foreman became a key part of my business life. He was a lighting and maintenance wholesaler and his clients owned their own companies. He had a stellar reputation as a no nonsense guy who could absolutely be trusted. He shipped products directly to our Argon customers and also mailed our invoices. Payments were received at a Post Office Box we set up in New Jersey. A flawless operation, right?

Wrong! I did not anticipate the consequences of the jealousy that was already running rampant among the sales people at Prospect. One weasel in particular, Norm Hausman, had his ear pinned to our door and was eavesdropping on Doug's and my

124

phone calls. He heard the end of my usual pitch when I said in what I thought was a low voice to the buyer, not to forget that the merchandise was coming from Argon Industries.

Without knocking, Norm waltzed into our office with his shit eating grin spread all over his face and announced that he knew we had formed our own company. Before I could say a word, he placed his index finger over his lips and shushed me. There was nothing I could say anyway. He had us by the balls. He promised to keep our secret if we walked him through the process of opening his own private company. Doug and I had no choice. We had to capitulate to this jackass knowing that if Donny and Steve ever found out, we'd all go down together.

Unfortunately, Norm the weasel was also a lapdog. He was the ass end of a partnership with Vic Perlman and firmly under Vic's orders, Norm dutifully stalked the hallway outside our office until he discovered the 'secrets' to our success and reported back to Vic.

With Vic in the picture, Doug and I needed to exercise caution. Vic thought of himself as a slick operator and always the smartest guy in the room. But in truth he was shamelessly arrogant and reckless; an ugly train wreck waiting to happen. He recently sidestepped a prison sentence when one of his many scams had blown up on him.

He had been making random calls to companies asking for the name of the person authorized to make purchases and then hanging up the phone. Without ever speaking with the authorized buyer, Vic would ship a case of trash can liners that cost him fifteen dollars. When he wrote up the order, instead of using a purchase order number which he obviously didn't have, he would indicate that the purchase was a verbal authorization from the legitimate buyer whose name he had obtained in the initial phone call. He'd mail the invoice for three hundred ninety nine dollars plus shipping knowing full well that most of those invoices would be paid because the cost was under five hundred dollars and no red flags would be raised.

Sooner or later, when some of the buyers discovered the inflated prices and demanded a refund, he would simply have the merchandise returned, but they were stuck with the shipping cost. Nevertheless, six or seven out of every ten companies he contacted actually paid the invoice so Vic would just continue shipping orders until the company caught on to the scam. Eventually, the postal authorities caught up with him and he shrewdly dodged the bullet by closing the company before they could file charges.

Vic was a salesman who didn't like making calls. He preferred to sit comfortably in his custom designed ergonomic leather chair with his feet resting lazily on top of his empty desk reading the sports page and listening religiously to the Howard Stern radio show. The only calls Vic ever made were to his bookie to place a bet or to order pizza.

Norm, on the other hand, was a workaholic. He was on the phone twelve hours a day. He started at eight a.m. East Coast time and continued after our office closed at five p.m. for another three hours taking advantage of the time difference with the West Coast until their offices closed. There were many times when I arrived at work in the morning and found Norm face down on his desk snoring away and those were the only times I saw Norm without the phone in his ear. Except when he was spying on me and Doug.

Their 'partnership' actually worked. It was far from fair and balanced, but Norm had no complaints. Vic would buy inexpensive Dunn and Bradstreet cards that featured only the company name, address, phone number and the total amount of the annual sales. The missing detail, of course, was the name of the buyer. Vic would give the cards to Norm, and Norm would make the cold calls. Vic would sit back and enjoy a fifty-fifty split on all the commissions Norm would receive from the sales he completed.

Norm was a great salesman, one of the best I've been around and their new company, Gemco Industrial, grew so quickly they left Prospect a couple of months later. Vic, however, could not leave quietly. He threatened to rat out me and Doug and make our lives miserable at Prospect. He laughed and gloated about how we would have to think about him every day and wonder if and when he'd reveal our little Argon Industry secret to Donny and Steve.

There was no way a prick like Vic could ever make me sweat or lose sleep. I formed Neptoon Industries as a subsidiary company of Argon for the sole purpose of raiding Vic's accounts. Neptoon was incorporated in California with an 800 toll free number. Our names did not exist on any paperwork whatsoever.

127

By the way Vic, your new company just got added to our Monday night trashing schedule, in fact, you jumped up to number one on the list. We hit Gemco's dumpsters three Mondays in a row and came up empty. I knew Vic was a clever and devious guy, but there was no way he was aware of our trashing exploits. They were dumping their trash somewhere else. But where?

The answer was simple. Harry the locksmith. I found him in the yellow pages. He advertised himself as the 'Key King' (who could go wrong with a name like that) offering cash discounts and a guaranteed fifteen minute arrival time. On two previous occasions, I had an issue with the lock on the front door of my house. The first time I needed to change the entire lock on that door and the second time I lost my key somewhere and figured he would have to change the entire lock again.

Harry was an honest guy. He said the lock was fine and I only needed a new key. Within minutes he produced a replacement key that worked perfectly.

Flash. The lightbulb in my head went off. Harry could make me a key to Vic and Norm's office. We could walk right in, make copies of their accounts and no one would be the wiser.

"Harry, my friend," I said. "How would you like to make an easy five hundred dollars?"

"I'd love to. What do you need me to do?"

"These two assholes that I used to work with stole some of our accounts and we want to get them back but they're locked up in

128

their new office. I need a key to get in. Is that something you think you could do?"

"No problem. Just tell me where and when."

Harry met me at Gemco Industries at two a.m. the next night. Again, it took him less than fifteen minutes to make a shiny new key which he handed to me with a knowing smile and said to give it a try.

I inserted the key, turned it and heard a familiar 'clicking' sound. I cautiously turned the knob and gently edged the door open just a crack.

"Holy cow Harry, you're the best," I said with a wink.

I quickly relocked the door and with a satisfied smile, handed Harry an additional five 'Benjamins' and thanked him sincerely for all his help.

He grinned and replied, "Mr. Newman it was my pleasure. If you ever need anything else, just give me a call."

The following Monday, after Doug and I completed our trashing rounds, I stopped the car in the parking lot next to Gemco Industrial. Doug had a perplexed look on his face. "What are we doing here? There's nothing in their dumpster."

I dangled the key in front of his confused eyes. "Right you are, but I just happen to have a key to the gold."

Doug's mouth opened slowly in utter disbelief. "No Scott, you can't be serious. We can't go in there. That's breaking and entering."

"Listen, you big pussy. It's called payback and that's not a crime."

"Well it is to the cops," Doug protested. "You've done some crazy things Scott, but nothing like this insanity."

"Listen to me for a second Doug. Vic screwed us over. He's been holding us hostage for two months now." I displayed the key again. "You're gonna need another safety deposit box at the bank to hold the cash we're gonna make from those accounts."

"I'm serious Scott. This is just plain stupid. What if we get caught? I don't want to risk losing everything and maybe even going to jail."

"Find your balls Doug. We are not gonna get caught. This is about revenge. Just think about all that money just waiting for us."

Thinking about the money somehow gave Doug the courage he needed to get out of the car. I slipped the new key into the lock and opened Gemco's door anticipating an alarm. Nothing. I chuckled out loud.

Yeah, Vic, you were right. I did think about you every goddamn day, but not out of fear. I just thought about the day I could wipe that high and mighty look off your fucking face. I eased the door open and marveled at all the file cabinets. It was going to be today.

Doug's eyes popped out of his head when he opened the first cabinet and saw nothing but paid up accounts. In less than a second he morphed from 'Chicken Little' into 'Rambo' on a mission. He loved the smell of money. We proceeded to carefully remove the files and make photo copies of the documents with the copy paper I brought along for the occasion, then meticulously returned the files to their original positions in the filing cabinets. We finished the drill in a little over an hour, double checked to make sure everything was in perfect order and withheld our victory celebration until our getaway car was a few blocks away.

HEH HEH HEH HEH HEH

Over the next week we worked Vic and Norm's accounts to the tune of seventy five accounts through Neptoon Industries. Screw Prospect. They weren't getting any of these primo accounts. After three weeks we closed a total of one hundred and fifty. It didn't take long for Vic and Norm to discover that a flood of their accounts was being sold by one of their competitors, Neptoon Industries.

Who the hell was Neptoon they wondered. Like Sam Ross from Supreme Lighting, Vic went ballistic. He knew this was not a coincidence so he actually stopped listening to Howard Stern for a few days, got off his ass and called everyone he could think of for information, but came up with nothing. Vic was so desperate he even contacted me to see if I knew anything about those lowlifes at Neptoon! I told him I was shocked and outraged by the audacity of those devious bastards and promised him I would do everything in my power to help track them down.

Sure thing Vic. I'll get right on it. I'm always happy to help out a backstabbing bastard like you.

I had created Neptoon Industries as a subsidiary of Argon to exclusively sell Gemco's accounts. Vic had no idea that in terms of sales, Neptoon basically functioned as a branch office of Gemco right under his nose. And once I sold Gemco's customers, I insured their loyalty by giving them gifts that Norm and Vic would never match. They were my guys now. They would never buy from Gemco again because no one could ever 'out gift' Scott Newman, the 'King of Benjamins'.

Doug and I cooled it for a couple of months, not only to let the shit storm die down, but to wait for good ol' Norm to replenish his accounts. That madman would probably be working the phones 24/7. We were cheering for him because little did Norm know, he was actually working for Neptoon Industries! Our next forays into Gemco's file cabinets yielded more golden accounts which we did not hesitate to harvest. Thank you, Norm! We'd love to give you a bonus, but...

Vic was unusually quiet. There was no more industry gossip regarding his maniacal obsession to hang the Neptoon assholes by their balls. Maybe Howard Stern got wind of Vic's theatrics and hired him to be part of his dysfunctional radio family where Vic could scream and rant to his heart's content. Whatever Vic was up to was no concern of ours so we hit his office again.

BEEP   BEEP   BEEP

The ugly drone of a security alarm almost knocked me over as I turned the key in Gemco's lock. Vic was up to something after all! Doug and I raced to the car and got the hell out of there. This party sure was fun and profitable while it lasted I commented to the empty passenger seat. Where was Doug? I saw him dive head first through the open window so I knew he must be in the car somewhere. I drove straight to Doug's house, parked the car in the driveway and found him in his usual fetal position, curled up in the back seat. I laughed out loud and bellowed, "Honey, we're home!"

We forgot about Gemco Industries, they were history. However, many months later, Gemco coincidentally came up in conversation with a Prospect part-time salesman, Ron Larson. Ron was a good guy and we started hanging out after work shooting the shit over a couple of beers. He owned a company that was going through an extended rough patch of declining sales and had a big family to support as well. He was struggling to make ends meet and really needed the Prospect job. Ron was curious about how I achieved my super 'bulber' status and really needed some advice.

At this point, I trusted Ron to a certain extent and considered him a friend. The 'trashing' scheme that Doug and I shared was sacred ground. We would never reveal our secrets, even under the duress of extreme physical torture. (Okay, Doug would fold before

133

they even touched him.) The Gemco story was harmless so I shared the Vic and Norm 'pay back' adventure with Ron.

Without revealing critical details, I said that when Vic and Norm worked for Prospect, they stole accounts from me and Doug. When they left to form Gemco, we saw the opportunity to get some accounts back from them. It was smooth sailing until they installed a security alarm system and without the code it was impossible to continue.

Ron's face turned bright red and his eyes bulged out of his head and for a long moment I held my breath. Was he going to blow up in anger? Was he experiencing a heart attack? Finally, he burst out laughing. "You gotta be kidding me. I know all about Gemco! I'm the one who installed their alarm system. That's what I do. That's my company!"

"That's your company?" I repeated as an incredulous grin spread across my face. "How would you like to become a one third partner for all the accounts we sell from Gemco Industries?"

"The code is 8641," Ron said without hesitation. "When do we start?"

We started that night and immediately hit a roadblock. They had changed the door lock too. No problem. A quick call to Harry the locksmith and a thousand dollars later, we had a new key. Ron punched in the code to disarm the security system and quickly inspected the office for other security devices. He gave us a 'thumbs up' and we were back in business or to put it another way, Norm was working for us again. Welcome back Norm!

Doug and I were thrilled to share a bit of our success with Ron. His life improved dramatically. He closed down his failing security alarm business and was working full time for Prospect. I remembered how Bob Rosen had gone out of his way to mentor me and share his industry knowledge that launched my 'bulber' career. I did the same for Ron, taking him under my wing and guiding him through the jungle of our business.

One of Ron's first learning experiences was with one of my biggest accounts, a steel company that did over a billion dollars in annual sales. The maintenance manager, James Tyler, called me and instantly began screaming so loud I didn't need to put him on 'speaker'. Ron and everyone else within a mile could hear him. He demanded to know why I was intentionally sending unauthorized orders at insanely inflated prices to his company.

"James," I calmly replied. "Your guy, Bill Walker, gave me the Purchase Orders and your accounting department always paid the invoices so it was fair for me to assume that Bill must have some kind of authority as a buyer."

"He doesn't have the authority to buy a bag of shit. I'm going to fire that son of a bitch and while I'm at it, I should call your boss to let him know that he should do the same to you. Your prices are absolutely insane and I'm sending the last two orders back to you."

"James, I can't take them back. It was special order merchandise, but I'll go ahead and discount the invoices twenty five per cent."

James was still pissed off, but at least he lowered the volume. "Okay fax it over to me and I'll take care of it, but don't you ever call my company again." I heard his phone shatter when he slammed it down.

Ron shook his head and remarked, "I guess that's the end of that."

"Oh no my friend, this might be the beginning," I said. "Never say never. We'll wait a couple of months and give this guy James a call like nothing ever happened. The worst he can do is hang up on me and break another phone."

Sure enough, when I called him two months later he answered. I greeted him with a warm good morning and said this was Scott over at Prospect. He didn't slam the phone down. I told him how much I appreciated his business and that I was gonna take good care of him, just don't forget me when something comes up. I mentioned that I would like to send ten crisp 'Benjamins' to his home address. He said okay and instantly gave me his home address. When that happens, you know he's in the game. He gave me a couple of Purchase Orders without even asking about prices. James no doubt realized that I was gifting his guy Ron and figured it was his turn to enjoy the benefits.

At the end of the day, James became one of my biggest 'whales' purchasing over forty thousand dollars worth of products a month. And the Priority Overnight envelope that routinely arrived every month at his home address usually contained at least forty freshly minted one hundred dollar bills from the 'King of Benjamins'.

HEH HEH HEH HEH HEH

Although things were going well and I was making more money than ever, I was restless. 'Thinking too much' as Amy phrased it. So I was thinking about my three largest accounts: the Ohio hospital, a national food wholesaler and a giant steel manufacturer. The plain and obvious fact that I was averaging almost one hundred thousand dollars a month in sales on these three accounts alone was a constant source of irritation. After deducting the cost of merchandise, gifts to the 'mooches' and my twenty four thousand dollar monthly salary, Steve and Donnie were making a net profit of over fifty thousand dollars per month on just these three accounts not to mention the hefty revenue they were receiving from all my other accounts.

Some of my best accounts were with my own company Argon. Why shouldn't all of my accounts be with Argon? It was time to cut the umbilical cord with Prospect and become completely independent. Nothing was going to stop me. The big question mark as usual was Doug.

Would he be willing to remove the safety net and walk the high wire act with me?

# Chapter Eight

## THE BENJAMIN KING

With apologies to Amy for 'thinking too much', the more I thought about it, the angrier I became. Doug and I had established and cultivated a massive number of valuable accounts without a *shred* of assistance from Steve and Donny. They were enjoying the lion's share of the profits that we generated. Screw that. Their 'contribution' consisted of an office, a phone and shitty leads that we had been ignoring for years. Time to bust a move.

"My mind is made up Doug," I proclaimed triumphantly at lunch. "We're leaving Prospect and devoting all of our time and energy to Argon and Neptoon and keeping ALL the profits for ourselves."

I was sure that Doug would enthusiastically agree with me and pound his first on the table declaring solidarity like a good teammate and business partner.

"No way Scott," he cried. "Are you completely out of your mind? How can I give up a six thousand dollar a week salary? How can YOU give up six thousand dollars a week? We have a great thing going here. We're on 'easy street'. Why do you want to wreck things?"

"I can't believe that after all we've been through and all we've accomplished that you are still afraid of your own shadow. For once take a look at the big picture. All you see is the bullshit salary you're making today. I see the future and what kind of mind-boggling money we would make tomorrow just by walking out the door today. This afternoon. Now. Come on Doug. I'm done with Prospect. I'm outta here."

"Before you do this," Doug pleaded. "Please let's sit down with Amy and Sheila and involve them in your decision. It's only fair."

I sighed and reluctantly agreed to his request. I didn't want to drag this thing out any longer. The four of us met at his house and of course Amy and Sheila agreed with Doug. How could I walk away from six thousand dollars a week? Easy.

"Remember 'Christmas in July' Amy? No one believed I could pull it off, but I kicked ass and now everyone uses that marketing term. When you doubted me, I promised you, I guaranteed you that it would be a success. I have the same feeling now about leaving Prospect. Forget the month of July. I'm telling you right now that every damn month of the year will be 'Christmas in July'."

Doug stared at the floor. Sheila stared at Doug. Amy put her arms around me and broke the silence. "Honey I believe you. I believe IN you. Let's do this. Bye bye Prospect."

Doug was not happy as I began laying the groundwork for my departure from Prospect. We knew that the second I quit, Steve and Donny would be furious and it would be a race to re-sell our accounts between Prospect and Argon. Doug would be on the hot seat. He would have to show sales results immediately because of his status as one of the top Prospect salesman. Donny and Steve would also distribute the same accounts to the entire Prospect sales force to insure victory. This was shaping up as a classic David versus Goliath business clash.

What Goliath did not anticipate was my plan. Obviously, Donny and Steve had no idea that Doug and I were partners in Argon so Doug concentrated his calls on the accounts that already had 'mooches' in place. He kept the orders and the gifts small and advised the 'mooches' to wait until the 'Benjamin King' called to take better care of him than Prospect ever could.

At the same time, I would be calling our Prospect accounts with the following pitch. "Good morning, it's your good buddy Scott. I wanted to touch base with you and let you know that I left Prospect and opened my own company called Argon Industries. That's great news for you because now I can take better care of you than I ever could at Prospect. Just do me a favor. If anyone calls you from Prospect, just tell them you're good and you don't need anything at this time. And don't mention Argon Industries. Trust me, the 'Benjamin King' will make it well worth it."

The 'Benjamin King' was now completely autonomous. I was in a position to implement the brilliant idea that I kept under wraps until the moment I could dedicate myself full time to my own company.

These were appetizers. I Priority Overnighted them to buyers and a couple days later I followed up with a phone call. It was very rare not to receive a healthy order.

Success meant going the extra mile with my buyers. I kept a record of their birthdays including their wives and children as well as anniversaries. And they never doubted that I would always take care of them on every major holiday.

Meanwhile, Doug and I agreed that all the Argon accounts we had opened together would continue to be split fifty-fifty along with the previously established Prospect accounts. However, every account I opened from now on was exclusively mine since I would be working Argon full time while Doug was still at Prospect collecting his comfortably secure salary.

The plan went into motion after Steve okayed my request for a week off so Amy and I could have a holiday in Florida. In reality, I spent the week in my Argon office and I hit as many of our accounts as possible because Steve would soon realize that a company called Argon was selling Prospect's accounts. The week passed quietly and profitably. I called Steve on the Monday I was scheduled to return to work at Prospect and told him this was important and to put my call on 'speaker' so Donny could hear what I had to say.

"I've been thinking about the staggering gap between your profits and my salary. It's like a big black hole that keeps expanding in your favor every day."

"Come on Scott," Steve groaned. "Not this shit again. Do you need another week off? Are you still in Florida?"

"No guys I'm actually sitting in my office. I didn't quite make it to Florida. I'm calling not only to thank you for all the shitty 'leads' you gave me while I was at Prospect, but to inform you that my new company will be enjoying all the spectacular profits from now on."

"You backstabbing piece of shit," Steve screamed.

I heard a gagging sound as Steve inhaled his cigar and started violently retching. My only regret was that I was not there to see his red face contorting in rage and gasping for air while Donny pounded his fist on Steve's back until he choked up the *shreds* of his mangled cigar.

They blew up like volcanos. The explosion of violent cursing and the shattering of furniture boomed throughout every office in the building and deep into the parking lot. Tough luck boys. How could you bastards not see this coming? Doug heard the fireworks and when he finally crawled out from underneath his desk, he called me and said I needed to find a new 'trashing' partner until the storm blew over.

Next man up was Fred. I knew him fairly well. He was my next door neighbor. When Fred lost his job as a telephone collector, I took him under my wing like Bob Rosen had done for me and offered to get him started as a 'bulber'.

His wife Rhonda, blew a gasket. She never needed a megaphone, her tirades were legendary around the neighborhood. Rhonda was a lot like *Old Faithful*, the famous geyser in Yellowstone Park that was guaranteed to erupt every couple of hours.

"You're a moron Fred. How can you even think about getting into that shady business. I don't trust that shifty Scott guy at all. I heard that he gives his customers 'gifts'. Everyone knows that's just a code word for cash. Mark my words Fred, some day that egomaniac is gonna get busted for his bribery schemes and we don't want to be anywhere near that mess."

Evidently, she didn't like me very much, but I convinced Fred to come on board anyway.

"For once in your life don't listen to her. You just lost your job, my friend. I guarantee this new job will pay off immediately. It's a telephone gig and the good news Fred is that no one will ever see your face so you'll never have to worry about the fact that you look like Shrek on a bad day. The better news is that you have a voice like James Earl Jones and you're gonna make more money than you ever dreamed."

Fred proved to be a great salesman. Even though he was making piles of money, Rhonda was constantly blaring like a fog horn about how he should be doing his job so I suggested that he visit the Mercedes dealership and give some thought to purchasing her a new vehicle. A couple days later there was a beautiful 450 SL parked in his driveway. Things were pretty quiet at Fred's house after that.

Like most of the enterprising salesmen at Prospect, Fred followed the same path of success and formed his own company, Welcon Products, while still working at Prospect. It didn't take long for Welcon to grow large enough to give Fred the confidence, not to mention the electric cattle prod from Rhonda, that he needed to leave Prospect.

When he proudly showed me the incorporation papers, I noticed that Rhonda was listed as one of the two officers of the company. So much for her contempt of our 'shady' business. I had a gut feeling there was a hell of a lot more to Rhonda than the screaming shrew act she put on for the neighbors.

When I asked Fred if he would be interested in 'trashing' with me, naturally he looked a bit confused not knowing what the hell I was talking about. But when I explained the details of the Monday night operation and the fact that these were not 'leads' but genuine accounts split fifty-fifty between us, he was thrilled to become my new 'trashing' partner.

It was the same 'trashing' drill with Fred. We would leave the 'useless' bags of shreds alone and cross those companies off our hit list. After we called it a night and Fred went home, I would, of course, go back to retrieve the shreds for myself. One night Fred was staring into an open bag of shreds and he suddenly thanked me for taking a big load off his mind.

"I sleep a lot better now Scott since I've been 'trashing' with you, I realize how important it is to shred all my documents.

Funny he should say that. Fred's shreds were the first bags I hit after saying good night to him. I knew he had golden accounts so I spent all night piecing his shreds together and immediately made phone calls starting the very next morning. Fred was aware of Argon so there was no way I could sell his accounts through that company. So all the sales were made through Neptoon Industries, the company I originally incorporated in California to sell Vic and Norm's Gemco accounts.

One Monday night before we started 'trashing', Fred was fuming with frustration. He was so angry he could hardly spit the words out.

"There's some asshole out there stealing from me Scott. It's some sneaky company in California that's selling the shit out of my accounts. Neptoon Industries. No one's ever heard of them. Those bastards only have a P.O. Box and a phone number that goes straight to voicemail. I never speak to a live person or receive a return phone call. I've asked all around and nobody knows anything. What the hell can I do?"

I tried to console him. "Remember Fred, this is a nasty business. You can't trust anyone. I'll ask around about this Neptoon company, but I don't think it'll do much good. You know how paranoid most people are."

A week later Fred called me and said he had solved the problem. He fired everyone in his office.

"It was a conspiracy Scott. My employees were all in it together. They were all goddamn traitors, every last one of them. From now on it's just me and Rhonda. She'll answer the phones, type up the orders, send out the gifts and collect the money. I'll do what I do best, selling all day and then take care of the shipping. You were right. You can't trust anyone these days."

Especially your wife, Fred. It was no surprise when they moved their company to a remote corner of New Jersey, far enough away so my 'trashing' days with Fred came to an end. From what I understood, they refused to hire new people and Welcon remained a two person enterprise. I figured that Rhonda was really running the company anyway and she had no doubt abruptly fired every last employee. It was obvious to me now that Rhonda was the power behind the throne. Fred was just the sales voice of their company. Oh well, no more 'trashing' with Fred and I soon forgot about them.

One day I received an interesting call from my product wholesaler, Buddy Foreman. He supplied most of the lightbulb telemarketing companies in the New York/New Jersey area. He would directly ship their orders so he had a list of all their customers' names, addresses, contact numbers, purchasing agents, and the products they were buying. Telemarketing industry owners were extremely paranoid about having their accounts stolen and Buddy had an impeccable reputation and was trusted by everyone. And Buddy trusted me.

"Something's come up Scott and it's important that I speak with you and Doug in person ASAP."

"No problem Buddy, but I think we need to leave Doug out of this for now. I'll explain later when I come by after work today."

I flew out of my office at five o'clock on the dot and rushed to Buddy's office because I knew whatever he wanted to talk about was going to be mind-blowing.

Buddy got right to the point. "Are you familiar with Philip Gardner?"

"Sure I am. He has the largest light bulb company in the tri-state area. He's making a ton of money."

"Right," Buddy continued. "Phillip's company brings in over one hundred and fifty thousand dollars in paid up accounts every Monday. He's doing over seven million dollars a year. He is very shrewd and doesn't trust anyone. He doesn't even buy his products from me."

I laughed. "Buddy if you can't be trusted then no one can."

"Listen Scott, this is what I found out. Philip does not allow his wholesaler to ship products directly to his customers. Instead they ship to Philip's warehouse and from there he ships to his customers. A brilliant plan so no one knows who his customers are."

"Wow Buddy, I'm impressed. That's some serious paranoia."

"There's more, Scott. He even hired his brother to manage the warehouse and the shipping. And on top of that, he gave him a percentage of the business to insure he wouldn't sell the accounts to a competitor. How's that for paranoia."

"What a shame. I'd love to get my hands on those accounts. They're worth millions."

"Very true Scott and here's the interesting part." Buddy broke into laughter. "Yesterday I got a call out of the blue from Chuck Harwell, Philip's top salesman. He wanted to speak with me confidentially and only in person. I gave him my word and assured him that my word was my reputation and that everyone knows my reputation speaks for itself."

Buddy could hardly contain his excitement. "Chuck came to my office and said he was going to open his own company while still with Phillip and do business on the side. Phillip buys his products from the wholesaler that Chuck obviously can't use without getting busted so he asked me if I would be interested in shipping and invoicing his accounts."

"And could you be trusted with those accounts?" I laughed out loud.

"Of course I could," Buddy chuckled. "I told him not to worry because he was in good hands."

"You're a righteous bastard Buddy and I got a feeling the best part of the story is yet to come."

"Right you are, my friend. He told me he had so many accounts already built up that he didn't want to start selling them until he had a chance to speak with me and set things up."

"So how did he get his hands on all those accounts?"

"This is the best part Scott. For the last three months he's been going through Phillip's dumpster every Monday night and taking the trash bags loaded with his paid up accounts. He literally has hundreds of good accounts ready and waiting to be sold."

150

I howled with laughter again. "Holy shit Buddy, now I understand why we couldn't find anything in Phillip Gardner's dumpster every damn time we checked. I finally gave up and crossed him off our list. That sly dog Chuck is 'trashing' too. I can't believe it."

"Yeah, Chuck's a sharp guy, but he's not the best 'bulber' in the industry, not even close. You're the man, Scott and that's only one reason why I'm talking to you. The other reason is that I believe you can be trusted and we'd make a great team. What I have in mind I'd only propose to you and Doug. I would like the three of us to open up our own lightbulb telemarketing company. We'll set up a New Jersey Corporation and a P O Box and have all the mail forwarded here in New York. And we'll get an 800 number that goes straight to voicemail. No one will ever find out that we are behind the company. What do you think?"

"What do I think Buddy? I think it's a brilliant plan, but I have three stipulations."

"Fire away Scott. I'm listening."

"First, Doug is still on the payroll at Prospect making his safe and secure six thousand dollars a week and there's no way he's ever gonna quit. And for that reason alone he would always be a weak link in our company not to mention a high risk to collapse under any kind of pressure and give us up in a heartbeat. He's afraid of his own shadow. I don't think we can trust him any more so screw him. He didn't have the balls to come with me as a partner and help build up Argon Industries full time so why waste our time with him now."

"Good point."

"Second, all the accounts that Chuck has stockpiled represent millions of dollars.

I want those accounts for our company. When he starts giving you his customers to ship, let's wait a month and then you can start slipping me twenty or thirty accounts a week that we can sell through our three companies."

"Three companies? What are you talking about? I was thinking that one company was a damn good idea."

"It is a good idea, but I have a better one and that's stipulation number three.

As you know, the multi-million dollar companies that I'm already selling have huge monthly maintenance supply budgets and they buy from several different venders. If we had more than one company then our customers could buy a variety of products through our separate companies and we could easily double and triple our sales.

Our buyers would love the option of spreading out several individual invoices from completely different companies rather than having one huge invoice go through a single company. Don't forget that our guys know they would be enjoying double and triple gifts from the 'King of Benjamins'. These guys are not stupid. They'll be on board before we can blink twice."

"Sounds like a great idea, but do you think it will work?"

152

"Let me give you an example. If one of our accounts is buying lights from 'Company A' with three invoices a month of three thousand dollars each that's nine thousand dollars a month. Now the same buyer could also purchase chemicals and cleaning products with separate invoices from 'Company B'. And then from 'Company C', he can purchase even more products such as tapes, trash can liners, shrink wrap and so on. That's potentially twenty seven thousand dollars a month. We've just tripled our sales by having three different companies."

"Wow, that's impressive, but what about incorporating three companies?"

"Simple. We incorporate them separately in California, Texas and Alabama. Our names will not appear anywhere. I'll set it up so Buddy Foreman and Scott Newman do not exist. We can establish a post office box address for each company in its respective state with a forwarding address to your office in New York. Each company will have an 800 number and I'll take care of printing three completely different looking invoices.

Trust me Buddy, we'll be making millions. Right now I have over twenty accounts that generate eighteen thousand dollars a month each through my two companies, Argon and Neptoon, That's a total of over three hundred and fifty grand a month. Imagine the money rolling in when we kick off our three companies. It's going to be crazy! So what do you think Buddy? Do we have a deal?"

Buddy leaped out of his chair and grabbed my hand and held it firmly. "Great minds think alike Scott. The first order of business is Phillip's accounts. Chuck hits Phillip's dumpsters around eleven p.m. on Monday nights."

"So I'll get there first, say around eight p.m.. We'll beat good ol' Chuck to the punch and grab all the gold and he won't have a damn clue."

HEH  HEH  HEH  HEH  HEH

Buddy gave me a strange look and I realized he was hearing Woody Woodpecker for the first time.

"You better get used to that Buddy. It's the Woody Woodpecker money making victory yell and whenever I hit a home run, it just comes out automatically. And you're going to hear it a lot because you and me are going to be insanely rich. I sell and you ship, now that's what I call a great team. Let's think of some names for our new companies!"

Together we came up with Transco, Reliance Lighting and Falcon Industrial Supply. It was time to rock and roll. We hired three ladies to work out of Buddy's office and represent each of our three companies. Their responsibilities included answering the phone and taking care of invoicing and collecting.

Doug continued to pound rocks at Prospect and collect his secure paycheck while giving me ten to twelve new accounts a week to sell through Argon. I was saddened and disappointed to think that Doug was not on board with me and Buddy. He was an incredible salesman but always seemed to be clutching his tail in fear like the cowardly lion in *The Wizard of Oz*.

A month went by and I started raiding Phillip Gardner's dumpsters while Buddy was filtering twenty to thirty accounts a week from Chuck's stash to me. These accounts were so lucrative and time consuming that I no longer had the opportunity to make my usual rounds of dumpster diving much less the chance to piece together any shreds. It was nuts how quickly our operation was exploding with success, but it tortured me to think about how much money we were passing up because I didn't have any time to cover all the bases. We could use some help.

I sat down with Buddy and explained our dilemma.

"I don't have the time to hit any other dumpsters or put shreds together and I hate the fact we're leaving piles of money on the table. We could hire a couple of guys to do that for us and pay them a grand a week in cash. That would free me up to do what I do best - sell, sell, sell - and roll in even more revenue for us, but the big problem is that I don't know anyone we could trust."

"No worries, Scott. Let's keep it in the family. We can trust my nephews. They would quit their jobs in one minute for a thousand dollars a week to work for me and they know if they ever said anything outside these walls, the consequences would be very unpleasant."

That's all I needed to hear. I figured the nephews would master the art of 'trashing' quickly and sure enough, during our first training exercise we discovered gold. I wanted to check out a new company that was doing great business called Monarch Industrial Supply. Their office was located in a commercial building that housed six different companies and they shared a giant sized dumpster. This would be a time consuming challenge to go through all the trash bags to identify and separate Monarch's. Another complication was the presence of a security guard who spent most of his time watching TV in a small booth not far from the dumpster. I realized this trashing mission would require special supplies so I hit Walmart and bought flashlights and three walkie talkies.

My plan was simple. One nephew would stay with the car while the other nephew crouched down next to the office building with a clear view of the guard booth. The dumpster was about the size of a one bedroom condo so I had no problem slipping inside and using my flashlight to go through the bags without attracting the guard's attention.

Communication with the walkie talkies was the key to the operation. We could not risk voice contact so we used a 'click' system. When we pressed down on the 'talk' button and then released it, there was a brief but distinct clicking sound. One 'click' meant someone was approaching or nearby and two 'clicks' indicated that the coast was clear again. Three 'clicks' was the signal that I had completed the mission and the nephew who had stayed with the car should go to the dumpster and help carry the bags while the other nephew remained at his lookout position.

The plan worked flawlessly and when we opened the bags in Buddy's office, there was the ultimate gold - perfectly intact note books of information containing company names, addresses, phone numbers, maintenance managers, maintenance supervisors and purchasing agents. This absolutely floored me because it also included the authorized buyers, the names of the 'mooches' who were not only taking gifts but the actual amount of the gift as well as their home addresses and cell numbers.

There it was, right in front of my eyes. Everything I'd ever need; all the information I had struggled every day to score and so many times fallen short. This was equivalent to being granted only one wish from a genie in a bottle. There were millions of dollars of unshredded accounts sitting there in one amazing trash bag. It was a 'bulber's' miracle.

HEH   HEH   HEH   HEH   HEH

And by the way, that was Buddy's Woody Woodpecker money making yell of victory that echoed throughout the office. He was now a true believer.

During the following weeks, I had the time to concentrate solely on sales. I was a virtual selling machine closing more sales that I'd ever done before. The nephews had been trashing on their

157

own for a couple of months when they found a gold mine of information in Phillip Gardner's dumpster - notebooks of priceless information similar to the Monarch find. The Phillip notebooks immediately yielded lucrative new accounts for us until one day our Transco receptionist called me and said there was a ranting maniac calling on the 800 number.

I took the call and it was Phillip Gardner screaming his brains out. "I don't know who the fuck you are but I know you're stealing my accounts. You're nothing but a piece of shit and if I ever find out who you are I will hunt you down like a stray dog and break every bone in your body and that's a promise."

"Hold on there, pal," I said calmly. "I don't know who the hell you are and I have no idea what you're talking about, but I thought you'd like to know that this call is being recorded. If you ever call here again and threaten me, I will have the FBI at your office in a blink of an eye. Then we'll see how many accounts you can sell from the prison cell you're sharing with Bubba and Billy Bob."

I never heard from Phillip Gardner again, but he did start shredding all his documents. No problem. Buddy's nephews just spent the extra time required to piece them back together and pass them on to me.

Again, I received a call from the Transco receptionist. This time it was Larry from Monarch on the line. I prepared myself for another deranged rant, the likes of Phillip Gardner, but I was momentarily taken aback when Larry began the conversation with a pleasant greeting.

"I don't mean to burden you with my problems, but your company is hitting my accounts really hard and I'm asking you for a favor. Could you have your 'lead' sources remove my company's name from their list. You'll still have tons of accounts from them and I'd really appreciate it if you could help me out."

"Not a problem Larry. I'll give a call to all my sources and if they have any Monarch accounts on their lists, I'll instruct them to just cross them off and that'll be the end of it. Does that work for you?"

"Fantastic Scott. You are a true gentleman. I can't thank you enough."

I hung up the phone and for a couple of minutes I actually thought about leaving the Monarch accounts alone, but at the end of the day, this is a competitive business and being Mr. Nice Guy does not pay the bills. Three weeks later, a Fed Ex package arrived at the office addressed to me. There was a thank you card that read - 'Please accept this gift with my gratitude for the trust and integrity we've recently shared'.

Inside was some kind of object tightly wrapped in several layers of tin foil. Why the tin foil? The horrible smell from a nasty, rotting dead fish was my answer. Of course, the head was missing so I wondered what psycho *Godfather* wannabe was responsible. The answer came quickly when the receptionist asked if I wanted to take a call from another raving lunatic named Larry from Monarch.

Collections were not a problem for the three companies I shared with Buddy but Doug and I were seriously falling behind with Argon's accounts. Neither one of us had the time to collect so I ran an ad in the paper and hired this guy named Melvin without properly vetting him. The sneaky son of a bitch quickly discovered that Doug was shuffling accounts from Prospect over to me at Argon and demanded that I double his salary for his silence. I fired that asshole in a New York second and completely forgot about it.

Melvin, however, figured his information was worth money to someone so he contacted Steve at Prospect and said he had inside information that was worth two thousand dollars. For several years, Steve had been itching to nail someone's hide to the wall. He had seen so much shit go down behind his back that two thousand dollars would be a bargain if the info was relevant. Melvin blabbed away like a six year old kid in the principal's office while Steve's face turned several shades of red as he listened to the weasel give us up.

"Did you know that Doug and Scott Newman own a company called Argon?" Melvin gloated. "Doug has been selling accounts for Argon while working under your nose at Prospect for at least a couple years."

Steve slapped a wad of cash on Melvin's chest and told him to get the hell out.

Steve and Donny called Doug into the office for his beat down. Doug told me later that the office was hotter than a sauna when he walked in and he instantly started sweating. They stared him down until Steve exploded. "You son of a bitch. How could you do this to us after all we've done for you? And you fucking did it under our roof."

I could picture the whole ugly scene as it degenerated into Doug's hell on earth. I could see him hemming and hawing, sputtering out his apologies, taking their shit without one single thought about fighting back or defending himself. The chump was probably on his knees begging those assholes for forgiveness. If I was there it would have started out as a nasty bar brawl and escalated into a no-holds-barred UFC cage fight with no referee to stop the carnage even after they submitted and begged for mercy.

Those greedy bastards paid us shit compared to the fortune they were making from our accounts that WE brought into their company. They should consider themselves lucky that we didn't quit and go out on our own a lot sooner. So screw them. I hope they choke on the money we brought into their company and I'd be out the door before they had the pleasure of firing me.

But no, that didn't happen. The unfair tag team match continued. Now it was Donny's turn to pummel Doug. "Stop your crying you piece of shit. We don't want to hear it. Be thankful I'm only firing your ass and not kicking it all over the parking lot. Go straight to your car. Everything in your office is now our property. Now get the hell out of here and tell that scumbag Newman to go fuck himself!"

Fortunately, Doug had a copy of all the Argon accounts safely tucked away at his house. He left Prospect without cleaning out his office and drove straight to Argon. I was surprised to see him but quickly guessed what happened by the wrecked look on his face. After he told me the story, I encouraged him to take the rest of the week off and get a fresh start on Monday. He just nodded and trudged back to his car.

I wasted no time clearing out all the paperwork from Transco, Reliance and Falcon Supply and returning it to Buddy's office where I could safely continue selling the accounts.


When Doug returned on Monday to the Argon office, he still looked like something the cat dragged in and I almost felt sorry for him. I was trying to cheer him up when the door blasted open and two giant goons stomped into our office. They were wearing black suits a couple sizes too small for them which made them look a little like cartoon bad guys, but it was a sobering sight to see their Glock nines holstered under their armpits and fully exposed for our viewing benefit. If their goal was to scare us shitless, they definitely succeeded.

The first WWF steroid giant grunted. "OK ass wipes, listen carefully. We know that you're stealing our accounts. We don't know how the fuck you're doing it and we don't even care. If we find ... "

I politely interrupted him and noticed the other goon giant had placed his hand on his gun. "We have no idea what you're talking

162

about. What's the name of your company so we can make some sense of this?"

"Sharpe Industrial Supply asshole, but you already knew that."

I turned to Doug and looked at him with bewilderment. He was frozen so solid he couldn't even shrug his shoulders.

I turned back to the first goon and tried diplomacy. "I think this is a misunderstanding. This is Argon Industries. Are you sure you have the right company?"

"We don't make mistakes," he snarled.

The irony of this nasty encounter was that we had truly never heard of this company and we certainly were not stealing their accounts.

"Look, I'm sure we're not selling any of your company accounts. We were not even aware that Sharpe Industrial Supply existed. I'll tell you what, if you can show us some of your accounts that you say we're selling, I promise we will never sell them again."

The talking goon formed the shape of a gun with his index finger and stuck it in my face. "We don't have to show you shit. Consider this visit a friendly warning. If you are unlucky enough to see us here in the future, then the chances are real good you won't be seeing us leave next time."

The goons left abruptly, slamming the door behind them. My heart was racing while Doug collapsed in his chair, white as a ghost. I grabbed a bottle of Jack Daniels from my desk drawer and filled a coffee cup to the top. I secured the cup in Doug's trembling hands and forced him to take a few gulps.

The color soon returned to his face and he tried to find his voice. "My nerves are shattered. I don't know if I'm coming or going anymore. I feel like I've been mugged ten times in the last week. I need a break so I don't have to deal with this never ending shit every day."

"Don't worry about it Doug," I reassured him. "Let's figure something out. I have a few ideas. How about you?"

"I just want to be fair Scott and not put all the work on you."

"It's not about fair. You've been through hell. What do you have in mind?"

"Well, for starters, I haven't been 'trashing' in a while and I just don't want to do it anymore."

"No problem. Anything else?" So sorry Doug, you've already been replaced.

Doug sighed and continued. "I would like to have more free time. I don't want to spend all day in the office."

"You know what Doug. Neither do I. We've built Argon into a great company. We're making tons of money so we don't have to work our asses off anymore. How about dividing the work day into two shifts. I'll open the office in the morning and work from 7:30 to 12:00 or 12:30 and then you can cover the afternoon and close the office at 5:00. So in case the goons come back, they can only get one of us."

164

A massive look of pained relief came over Doug's face as he managed to laugh. "I'm not worried about them. They'll probably show up during your shift in the morning."

I laughed. "That's the spirit, Doug. Go on home and relax. I'll guard the fort the rest of the day. I'll see you tomorrow."

After Doug left it was my turn to feel relieved. With this new arrangement I could spend all afternoon at Buddy's selling the hell out of all our accounts for our three companies.

Buddy's nephews, however, presented a different kind of problem. A profitable one. They had been 'trashing' like gangbusters and bringing in tons of 'paid up' accounts and putting together so many shreds that I had no time to call all of these accounts. Buddy and I decided to bring on board another family member only this time it was from my family tree, my nephew, Justin. He had established his own telemarketing company a few years ago and built up a sales force of seven very productive 'bulbers'. He was the perfect choice to fulfill the next stage of my ultimate goal: running a multi-million dollar operation with annual revenues of over twenty five million dollars.

Justin enthusiastically agreed to become a one third partner with Buddy and me. He would keep the accounts he had already established and we would do the same with ours, but for all the accounts that we gave to Justin, the profits would be split in thirds. Buddy's warehouse was huge and several offices were quickly constructed to accommodate our new sales force. They were swamped from day one with mountains of accounts to re-sell because Buddy's nephews had perfected 'trashing' to a fine science and were assembling massive amounts of shreds at lightning speeds.

Justin and his guys were very good sales people, but I wanted to launch them to the next level so I called a sales meeting to establish the guidelines, principles and strategies that defined our three companies.

"Gentlemen, I am going to share with you the sales strategy that made me the 'King of Benjamins'. If you follow these very simple concepts, I guarantee that your sales record will sky rocket."

Holding the fake 'Benjamins' high in my hand, I proclaimed that these were 'gold'. I passed around a couple samples to each guy and waited for the emotional impact to register.

"What are you feeling right now fellas?"

Justin exclaimed, "I can't wait for the real ones to come."

"That's exactly how the buyer feels and now he can't wait to hear from you because just like it says right there on those beautiful Benjamins, 'the real ones are on the way'. When was the last time a buyer was looking forward to a phone call from you? You just achieved the impossible. You already sold the guy without even opening your mouth.

Let's say Valentine's Day is coming up. You send the buyer some fake Benjamins in a Two Day Priority envelope. The day after it arrives while the image of the money is still fresh in his mind, you give him a call. Ask him if he has a pen so he can write down the tracking number for the Priority Overnight envelope containing the real Benjamins. Do you think he's gonna decline or give you some lame excuse about why he can't give you an order right now? Do you really think he's gonna tell you to call back in a month or so? After he writes down the tracking number then you TELL him the details of the order. You do not ASK him if he needs anything because once he jots down the Priority tracking number, the order is automatic.

Everyone should have a big calendar book with plenty of writing space for each day of the week. Why? Because you're going to start with all the major holidays and make a note to call your guys one week before the actual holiday and remind them that you are going to take very good care of them. For every buyer, you need to mark down their birthdays, their wives and children's birthdays, anniversaries, graduations, weddings and any other major event in their lives using the same strategy you employed for holidays.

This is the masterplan for success, my friends. It takes a lot of planning, hard work and staying on top of things, but no other company does this. This is how I became the 'King of Benjamins' and if you follow these strategies religiously then at the very least, you can become a 'Prince of Benjamins' and wealthy beyond your dreams."

Our small-scale sales force of nine people was selling three hundred accounts a week to the tune of half a million dollars. That's two million a month or twenty four million a year - my goal!! We were easily out selling companies with seventy five sales people. How was this possible? It's not rocket science. We did not make cold calls. We did not scour through manufacturers' catalogs. We did not speak with receptionists who filtered calls and functioned as roadblocks to authorized buyers. We did not waste our time chasing useless 'leads' like those Steve and Donny passed out at Prospect. We had direct access to buyers. And what buyer is going to refuse a gift from the 'Benjamin King', the guy who went *from shreds to riches.*

HEH  HEH  HEH  HEH  HEH

One day, Buddy got an unexpected phone call from one of his guys on the street. Word through the grapevine was the FBI was snooping around asking a lot of questions about the telemarketing

168

lightbulb industry. Buddy was very concerned for me and Doug because a lot of people were aware that we owned Argon and a lot of people were not fond of us at all.

He suggested that we remove all the paperwork from the Argon office that might potentially incriminate us in any way.

"No worries, Buddy. Argon is a clean operation. Doug and I are not doing anything illegal."

"That doesn't mean shit to the government," Buddy cautioned. "Those bastards can do whatever the hell they want and if they want you, they got you. And there's not a goddamn thing you can do."

I didn't share this tidbit with Doug. I didn't want to be responsible for his heart attack. Little did I know, however, that we would soon have some unwelcome visitors that would make the steroid goons look like school boys.

# Chapter Nine

# STUNG BY THE RAID

Thanks to Rhonda, the FBI rumor became an ugly fact within months.

My suspicions about her running the show at Welcon proved to be true. I had known Fred for a long time and somehow he failed to mention that she was a Certified Public Accountant from a clan of CPA's: mom, dad, brother, sister and who knows, maybe the entire family tree was full of them. She also had an MBA from some fancy Ivy League school like Harvard or Yale. She was definitely a wolf in sheep's clothing and Fred, although he was a great salesman, was evidently along just for the ride.

Rhonda was operating Welcon out of a remote corner of North Jersey, far enough away from New York where she could put her scheme into motion without drawing attention from the hub of the telemarketing lightbulb industry. She wanted to create a huge advantage over the rest of the competition so she formed a new company called 'Universel'. Why *Universel*? Because the largest maintenance industrial wholesaler in the country was a multi-million dollar giant called Universal Industrial Supply. She simply changed one letter in the spelling of the name: the 'a' became an 'e'. She even printed up the invoices to look almost exactly like Universal's. It was a brilliant plan from the mind of a Harvard graduate that was absolutely foolproof...

Over ninety per cent of all companies in the United States buy a significant amount of their maintenance supplies from Universal so cashing in on their coattails was a walk in the park. It worked like a charm and over the following year, business was great. Their calls were accepted by almost every buyer, maintenance manager, purchasing agent and warehouse manager because all of them assumed it was the real Universal company that they were giving their orders to.

Eventually, the genuine Universal company discovered the scam. Irate customers began flooding corporate headquarters with complaints about a company called 'Universel' pretending to be Universal and charging grossly inflated prices and sending invoices that looked identical to the authentic Universal paperwork.

Universal's legal department sent a boatload of evidence to the FBI and it wasn't long before a warrant was issued. An FBI team, led by Agent Gloria Perez, conducted an unusually quiet raid on 'Universel's' office and confiscated all of Fred and Rhonda's paperwork and shut them down. The raid was successful on many levels. First, absolutely no one in the lightbulb industry was aware of the raid. Second, they successfully scared the shit out of Fred and Rhonda and offered them an undefined 'sweet deal' if they cooperated with the sting the Feds would soon be putting into motion.

When Agent Perez put the hammer down on Fred and Rhoda, she informed them that Universal was pressing charges and they were both looking at fifteen to twenty years in a Federal Penitentiary in addition to the government appropriation of all their assets. Whether there was any truth to that or not was completely beside the point. The Feds had a vice grip on their balls.

Sitting uncomfortably in the cramped office of Agent Perez, Fred and Rhonda listened as the riptide of bad news sucked away any hope of clemency. "Fraudulent Misrepresentation is an automatic prison sentence," she stated flatly. "You two committed business fraud in epic proportions, bilking unsuspecting buyers out of hundreds of thousands of dollars if not millions with your copycat company."

"With all due respect, Agent Perez, there is no need to exaggerate the situation," retorted Rhonda defensively.

"Take a good look around you," Perez suggested.

The floor of Agent Perez's office was overflowing with towering stacks of paperwork that almost touched the ceiling. If someone slammed the office door it would easily trigger an avalanche of documents that would surely bury them alive.

"That's called 'evidence'," Perez casually commented and paused to let her words sink in. "And we have not even begun to calculate the monetary compensation to satisfy the injured parties."

Fred and Rhonda stared hopelessly around the office and finally at each other. Fred shrugged his shoulders and said nothing. Rhonda returned Perez's gaze and recognized that she had met her match and silently surrendered, at least for the moment.

"We're going to set up a sting and you two will be front and center of the operation. This is how it's going to work. You're going to contact all the light bulb companies you know and tell the owners that you are retiring from the business. So how many owners do you know?"

"Not very many," Fred said apologetically. "The people in this industry are extremely paranoid. No one trusts anyone. Stealing accounts happens all the time so there's almost no contact with other companies."

"I need a number," Perez said impatiently.

"Okay. Maybe three or four," Fred offered timidly.

"You can do better than that Fred and think about this. The more companies you give us, the more we will be inclined to reduce your prison time and fines."

"All right. I know a few guys from Prospect when I worked there and a couple golfing buddies. I'd say in the neighborhood of ten, eleven, twelve."

"That number works for me," Perez was satisfied. "We know you've been very resourceful, Rhonda, parlaying your company profits into investments that have yielded millions and are safely tucked away in off shore accounts. And we'll be looking into that soon enough.

Anyway, here's the story you're going to tell. You're retiring from the business and closing your company because you've made millions on Rhonda's outside investments. You've worked hard enough so now you're going to enjoy the rest of your lives drinking Mai Tai's on the beach of a warm and sunny Hawaiian island."

Fred actually cracked a thin smile as he imagined himself lounging on the beach. Rhonda continued to stare impassively at Agent Perez.

Perez continued with the story line. "You have some great accounts from all over the country and you're willing to hand them over to each of these target companies on the condition that they give you a percentage of their sales on the back end when the invoices are paid. Offer each company the same five accounts to begin with and if they're satisfied with the sales results, remind them you have many more accounts available to re-sell."

Fred lost his faint smile and shifted uneasily in his chair. He knew he was the one who would be making those calls.

Agent Perez continued to nonchalantly recite the script she had memorized. "We are going to create what appear to be five legitimate companies located in five different states. Each company will have its own bank account, a physical address to receive merchandise and a phone number with an area code matching the state. When any of the target light bulb companies contact any of those five telephone numbers, the call will be forwarded to an FBI office in New Jersey where an FBI agent will be on the other end of the line posing as a buyer and recording the conversation. When the gift is offered, the agent will give out a home address just like a typical 'mooch'."

Fred was drenched in sweat. Rhonda folded her arms and scolded him. "There's no way you're getting out of this Fred so quit fidgeting and suck it up. You know that no one is going to compare notes. They will be thrilled to have those accounts all to themselves thinking that no one would ever be the wiser."

"Listen to your wife," Agent Perez advised as she looked skeptically at Fred. "There is absolutely no reason for these target companies to doubt the legitimacy of our bogus companies. All the invoices will be paid on a timely basis and every gift will be accepted without question. We want the target companies to sell the sting companies at least three or four times and of course, every word will be on tape."

"Okay Ms. Perez, if we agree to do this, what's our part of the so called 'deal' look like?" Rhonda asked coolly.

"If you fully cooperate and there are guilty pleas and/or convictions, enough so that we can consider this sting a success, then both of you will serve a maximum of one year each and only pay a hefty fine."

"Hold that thought Agent Perez. Let's continue this conversation at another time when our lawyer can be present to verify all of this with a written agreement. Until that happens, Fred won't be making any phone calls. I assume we still have the right to an attorney?"

"Oh absolutely," chuckled Agent Perez. "That's how the system works."

A week later, the phone calls to the target companies were scheduled to begin and the first call was directed to me. Fred was mulling over the list of phone numbers shaking his head with indecision when Rhonda's finger stabbed a name on the paper - Scott Newman.

"That son of a bitch is your first call," she commanded.

"Come on Rhonda," Fred protested. "We owe him. Scott went out of his way to get me into this business after I lost my other job. Why is he even on this stupid list?"

"We're going down Fred, remember? And how far down depends on how many owners we give to the Feds. That means we're going after everyone, especially Newman. I just wish I could be there when Agent Perez busts into his pretentious Central Park office and wipes the smirk off his face."

Fred knew he couldn't win the fight so he geared up for the call.

"Scott! How are you buddy, it's Fred," he expressed with his usual telephone charm.

"I'm good Fred. Great to hear from you. It's been a long time."

"Listen Scott, I finally got out of the business. I'm actually retiring, you know, starting my golden years about twenty years early. Rhonda made some great investments and we have enough money now so I can quit killing myself at work."

"No kidding," I exclaimed. "That's great news Fred. What are your plans? You're not going to hang around Jersey are you?"

"No, no, we loved Hawaii on our last vacation so that's where we're headed as soon as I wrap things up here. Anyway, I was looking over these boxes of accounts and there are some really good ones here and I think it's a shame to waste them. I know that you and Doug are fantastic 'bulbers'. No one in the business is better than the two of you. So I was thinking instead of letting these accounts collect dust, maybe you'd want to sell them. I'll give you a few to start and if you're happy with the results, let me know because I have several more available to re-sell. All I ask for is twenty per cent on the back end when the companies pay their invoices."

"Are these 'leads' or 'paid up' accounts? You know I don't waste time with 'leads'."

"No worries, Scott. These are genuine accounts that are already established with 'mooches', in fact, these guys are 'whales'. These are my biggest accounts and you'll sell everyone and make a shitload of money. I'll fax over five accounts to start with. You have nothing to lose. Are you interested?"

Fred was not kidding. The fax had all the information we needed to sell these five companies including the products they purchased, the gifts they received and the home addresses of the 'mooches'. They were the easiest sales we ever made. Too easy my gut told me, but I ignored it.

On one of my calls I spoke with the new maintenance manager. He mentioned that the previous manager was no longer with the company and he was now authorized to buy. (As I look back today and replay that phone call in my head, I still can't believe the 'new' manager was actually an FBI agent. Hell's bells, every goddamn call I made was to a Fed fronting for those five 'sting' companies.)

The 'new' manager sounded very positive on the phone so I pitched him a gift and told him it was a thank you for all his past business. He was very gracious and expressed how much he appreciated it. He said he needed some light bulbs and asked the price of a case of four foot fluorescents. I quoted a dollar figure that he said was a little high, but quickly decided to make the purchase when I mentioned the 'seven year, two for one' replacement guarantee for any burned out bulbs.

Doug and I resold those five accounts several times over the next few months making a nice profit with the large orders and 'paid up' invoices. We didn't know at the time that we were not the only beneficiaries of Fred's 'generosity'. There were eleven other light bulb companies selling the same five accounts.

An ear splitting boom from a battering ram shattered the front door of my office suite into splinters and a dozen FBI agents charged through the opening, peeling off to the left and right, flooding the reception area and the open work spaces.

Dressed in full combat regalia, the agents were prepared to engage and defeat any well armed and hostile resistance force. Some were wearing green body armor and Kevlar helmets and toting AR15's with Glock side arms.

Waving a warrant above her head was the lead agent. "My name is Agent Gloria Perez and this is a raid. There is an ongoing FBI investigation into the lightbulb telemarketing industry. We need to speak with Scott Newman and Doug Kaufman of Argon Industries."

"I'm Scott Newman what's this about?"

"Mr. Newman, we are not closing down your business. We have a warrant to search the premises and confiscate any and all evidence that we deem pertinent to our investigation including all paper work and computer hard drives. You may come by our regional office anytime during business hours and make photo copies of your documents for one dollar a copy. Is Mr. Kaufman here?"

Paralyzed by fear, Doug was escorted by two agents into the lobby.

Agent Perez presented the warrant to Doug. "Mr. Kaufman, do you understand why we are here?"

Doug just shook his head 'no' and looked at me for support.

"Relax buddy, this is some kind of mistake. We'll sort it out. Let's hear what the agent has to say," I said calmly.

"Like I said, we are not closing down your business. You are free to carry on during the investigation. In the meantime, send all your employees home because we're going to be here all day. They may return tomorrow."

I walked Doug to the opening that only a few minutes ago was the front door. He watched in misery as the agents lugged boxes away and mumbled, "They're taking everything Scott. They're here for my money"

"They can't take your money Doug, not unless you're dumb enough to give it to them. Just keep your mouth shut."

"Nah man, that's why they are here. This is more than just an investigation."

"You're just a little paranoid Doug. Relax. They're not after your precious money. Don't take this so personally. Maybe Buddy was right when he warned me that the FBI was snooping around.

This might be an industry wide investigation with several other companies going through this same raid bullshit."

"I don't care about the other companies. I care about me. I don't want to lose everything I worked for. That money is more than thirty years of my life."

"Doug, buddy, forget about your goddamn money for a second and take a look around you. We built this business together and no matter what happens with this investigation, we're going to fight them every step of the way."

Later that evening, Amy and I went to Doug's house to sort things out. Doug was a basket case. "I can't do this anymore. This investigation is not going away. What if this is a trap and every sale we make from now on is used as evidence against us. We have plenty of money so let's just stop now and close down Argon."

"Okay Doug, whatever you say," I reluctantly agreed. All four of us sadly accepted the end of our great run with Argon.

Okay Doug, whatever you say. If you only knew that two years ago, Buddy and I formed three separate companies just for a chicken shit occasion like this when I knew you'd quit on me.

"Argon is history," I informed Buddy. "We got raided by the Feds and Doug quit on me. The only paperwork in that office was Argon's and Neptoon's so while this investigation drags on, I'll be selling the hell out of our other three companies."

"You weren't the only company to get raided Scott. They nailed eleven other companies besides you."

"Holy shit," I gasped, "this is a big time sting operation."

"Yeah it sure is," Buddy agreed. "It's better that Argon and Neptoon are dead. Thank God we operated Transco and our other two companies out of my office. The FBI has no clue about us and no one in the industry knows that we are Transco, Reliance and Falcon. Our companies can't be traced back to us because we covered all our bases. Looks like we are safe."

"I hope you're right Buddy".

The investigation crawled along for months and Doug was no longer the ball and chain holding me back. I proceeded full steam ahead working out of Buddy's office, far from the probing eyes of the FBI.

Staying in touch with Doug was painful and I kept our conversations to a minimum and limited to updates on the investigation. It was exhausting to listen to his constant moaning about going to prison and the hand wringing about the Feds probably taking all his money. Usually he had very little to say and claimed there wasn't much of anything to report on his end and that was fine with me because I knew he was teetering on the edge of a complete nervous breakdown. I figured it was best to leave well enough alone. Or so I thought at the time.

I was confident the FBI investigation would eventually fizzle out. We had done nothing illegal. 'Gifts' and 'back end' deals were common business practices in every industry. Capitalism is what makes the economic world go around, right? I honestly believed there would be no indictments and that Doug just worried about monsters that didn't exist.

It was easy to put Doug and the FBI out of my mind and concentrate completely on work. Then one day Doug called me on my cell phone and I realized we had not spoken for over two months.

"Scott I'm so sorry," Doug sputtered as he cried and choked on his words. I couldn't understand a thing he said.

"Slow down Doug," I said patiently. "Take a deep breath and start again."

"I'm sorry. I had to do it. I had no choice."

"Do what? What are you talking about?"

"I pleaded guilty," Doug sobbed.

I couldn't believe what I was hearing. I exploded. "You did what?"

"They threatened to take all my money if I didn't cooperate."

"Fuck your money. What do you mean by cooperate?"

"They made me plead guilty to mail fraud and money laundering and to testify against you if you don't plead guilty too."

"You stupid piece of shit. We're not guilty of anything. We were supposed to stick together on this and you took a bullshit plea. Are you out of your mind? We never laundered any money. How could you plead guilty to that?"

"The government has all of the evidence. They told me to plead guilty or spend the next ten years in prison."

"They have no evidence you moron. They are desperate. They couldn't find any evidence to support these bullshit charges. Mail fraud? Money laundering? Are you kidding me Doug? They're making it look like we are dirtbag drug dealers. You just screwed us both."

"I know, I know. Scott please, just listen to me. I'm begging you not to go to trial. The government will make me testify against you."

"You know what Doug, you always told me that I'm a true friend and that you would never be able to get through this investigation without me. So now to save your own cowardly ass you sold me down the river. What kind of friend would do that?"

Doug choked up again. "I'm so sorry."

"Yeah Doug, you got that right. You are sorry. A sorry back stabbing son a bitch!"

I looked at my phone in utter disbelief and clicked it off and that's the last time we ever spoke.

How low can a weasel go? Doug actually believed the government would never confiscate every dollar of his assets so he agreed to wear a wire and contact two former Prospect salesmen who had moved on to become owners of their own companies. They assumed the innocent lunches with Doug were just friendly get togethers. They had no idea they were being set up and betrayed by a rat. These 'casual' conversations were recorded and eventually used as evidence to put both of them away for three years each.

With an indictment hanging over my head, I continued to sell the Transco, Reliance and Falcon accounts like a mad man. I didn't know how long it would be before they arrested me so I worked almost around the clock to sock away as much money as I could for Amy and our children and probably a defense lawyer or two because there was no way in hell I was going to plead guilty. Let's go to trial you government bastards!

Meanwhile, Doug the tightwad, ignored one of the top criminal law firms in New York (their offices occupied the entire floor above ours in the Central Park building) and contacted a lawyer named Gil Manford that he had seen on a billboard to represent his interests against the FBI. Doug's mission was protecting his two million dollars in investments and the half million in cash stowed in a safe deposit box. He was naively confident that his two-bit lawyer could protect his assets. Mr. Manford was quite proud of himself for negotiating a 'killer deal' with the government on Doug's behalf.

"No jail time, Doug," exclaimed Manford triumphantly. "All you have to do is surrender the two million in investments to the government. They, in turn, will reimburse the victim companies that you overcharged. That's more than fair."

"I can't give up my investments. I've been saving for over thirty years. That's my retirement money. How can the government take that? How am I supposed to live on nothing?"

"Would you rather be in prison? This is really a no brainer Doug."

"That is so messed up."

"Your choice my friend. Otherwise, they guaranteed ten years behind bars."

"Okay, okay," Doug shuddered at the thought of prison. "Just get it in writing."

"They can't put anything in writing at this time, but they promised to strongly advise the judge to give you a 'downward departure' (no jail time) in exchange for your cooperation in returning the profits you obtained by laundering money."

Doug was too stunned to say anything.

Manford bulldozed ahead. "They also want you to testify against Scott Newman if he goes to trial and to continue wearing a wire and record all the conversations you have with any other lightbulb companies."

Doug buried his head in his arms and hoped it would all just go away.

Who was Gil Manford really working for? I found it very hard to believe that Mr. Manford was actually representing Doug's interests. Two million dollars is a huge chunk of money and from what I heard later through the grape vine, none of the companies that had purchased from Doug and me never received a penny in compensation. It would not be out of the ordinary for Mr. Manford to receive a five to ten percent 'finders' fee from the government for his efforts in talking Doug out of that kind of money with no written agreement. Not bad for a low rent bankruptcy lawyer.

All was quiet for a few weeks until one morning my phone rang at six a.m. and aroused me out of a dead sleep. No one ever called me at that ungodly hour. Except the FBI.

"Mr. Newman, this is Special Agent Gloria Perez with the FBI. We have a warrant for your arrest. Your house is surrounded. Are you dressed?"

"No, I'm not. Why are you at my house? My family is here. What's wrong with my office? What ever happened to the option of turning yourself in without the drama?"

"You have ten minutes to get dressed and then we're coming in."

Exactly ten minutes later there was a knock at the door. I immediately opened it before they could break it down and Agent Perez marched right in followed by five agents decked out in combat gear.

Broadcasting the breaking news so all the neighbors could hear and waving the warrant like a victory flag, Agent Perez proudly announced, "Mr. Newman, the United States government has issued a warrant for your arrest."

She read me my rights and in full view of my anxious wife and terrified young son. Another agent instructed me to place my hands behind my back and quickly handcuffed me. Two more agents linked their arms through mine and escorted me out the door. I felt like I was trapped in a bad movie. When I turned my head and called out to my wife, "Don't worry honey, call our lawyer. Everything's gonna be OK."

The view of Central Park from the back seat of my limo was always spectacular, however, it was not quite the same from the back seat of a raven black SUV moving with purpose in the center of a caravan of identical black SUV's. It was an exhibition of flashing police lights and muted sirens assuring the community that public enemy number one had been captured. I was handcuffed and wedged between two burly agents who no doubt moonlighted as body guards to some New York celebrity or thug.

"Looks like you guys finally caught Al Capone," I commented to Agent Perez.

"He was from Chicago. This is New York," she responded icily.

"Are you guys aware that my last name is Newman, not Gambino or Gotti," I offered, attempting to lighten the somber mood.

No talking, no smiles, no jokes. This was serious business. Bail was set at one million dollars and Amy paid the ten percent bond in cash. Yes Doug, I have a safety deposit box too, except the whole world doesn't know about it. My attorney, Paul Arnett, actually specialized in criminal defense not bankruptcy and was present at the initial hearing.

There were two prosecuting attorneys. Why were there two lawyers I wondered? Are my alleged crimes so heinous that the government needs two lawyers to secure my conviction so the streets of New York remain safe and its citizens can sleep peacefully at night?

The black prosecutor was named Samuel Wilson and the white guy was Ronald Combs. This integrated attack team would certainly impress the jury before a word was spoken. Even though I pleaded 'not guilty' to the charges, the damage was already done. Doug had already caved in and agreed to testify against me.

The hell with Doug. My mind was made up. I was going to trial. The government wanted to avoid the time and expense of a trial because they thought it was a slam dunk case. They assumed I would jump at their generous offer of only three years in federal prison. When my lawyer relayed the government's offer, he warned me that if I was convicted at trial, it could be a sentence of six to ten years. Amy begged me to take the deal. She said three years was better than risking six to ten years. I told both of them that I understood their concerns, but the bottom line for me was simple: I didn't do anything illegal. These were bullshit charges and I intended to prove my innocence. We're going to trial.

Over the next few weeks I was required to spend most of my time at FBI headquarters with Mr. Wilson, Mr. Combs and Agent Perez. I thought I was in the movie *Groundhog Day* because every day it was the same thing. They tag teamed and badgered me repeatedly with the same questions. My attorney assured me this was part of the legal process and cooperating would make life easier. They constantly shuffled through the piles of Argon's paperwork and played the tapes of my conversations with buyers believing that would somehow intimidate me into a confession.

They were barking up the wrong tree yet again. I said nothing incriminating on those tapes. It was my typical sales pitch. If the buyer (FBI Agent) asked for prices, I didn't lie or bullshit, I gave him the prices. If he thought it was too high, I'd thank him for his time, ask him to think it over and if he changed his mind, then give me a call.

The three of them took turns asking the same questions. "Mr. Newman why don't you make it easier on yourself and take the deal we generously offered you or the deal is off the minute we go to trial. You already know what's going to happen. There's no way a jury will find you innocent."

I listened to this speech in silence for over a month and finally spoke up. "Gloria (I called all three of them by their first names on purpose) let ME tell YOU what's going to happen. You know this is a great story. I am going to win my trial, write a bestselling book which will then become a blockbuster movie. This is exactly the kind of David and Goliath story that Hollywood loves. So Gloria, what actress would you like to play you in the movie?"

A huge grin spread across her face. "Angela Bassett would be perfect," she heartily laughed. "Hey Sam," turning to Wilson. "Mr. Newman's going to make a movie about us. What actor would you like to play you?"

Wilson eagerly joined the fun and replied, "Morgan Freeman. Mr. Academy Award!"

Gloria rolled with the amusement of the moment, "How about you Ron?"

191

"It has to be an exceptionally handsome guy like Al Pacino."

Ha ha ha. They all thought it was a big joke, but at least for me it was a good break from the relentless barrage of questioning. The real joke was on them. They had no idea that every day as soon as I escaped from their office, I went straight to my own office at Buddy's and sold the hell out of the endless supply of my lucrative accounts making more money than they would ever see in their 'set for life' government jobs.

I had a bad feeling the government was unfairly stacking the deck against me so I hired another ace criminal attorney, John Roberts, to join our team. I felt we needed more fire power as the trial date neared since prosecutors Combs and Wilson were becoming more aggressive during what was supposed to be routine questioning at FBI headquarters.

They were no longer offering a three year prison term for my guilty plea, they were demanding it. Evidently, I had become a giant pain in the butt to the higher powers of government and the pressure to avoid a trial had significantly increased. Whoever the schmuck was that assured them I would cave in like Doug was probably sweeping floors on the night shift if he still had a job.

Leon Altman was one of my closest friends. Amy and I spent a lot of time hanging out with him and his wife Marsha. They owned a beautiful home not far from us and also had a cozy beach house on the Jersey Shore. I had taken him under my wing at Prospect and eventually convinced him to start his own company. He and Marsha operated their lightbulb business out of their home with no sales people or employees, just the two of them listed as owners of the corporation.

Leon and Marsha were raided at their home by the FBI the same day I was raided at my office. Ten agents dressed for combat, poured out of four SUV's, blasted the front door down and roared into their house with guns drawn. Their two young daughters were in the kitchen eating breakfast just before leaving for school and were utterly terror-stricken. They were eight and ten years old. And no, the government does not provide counseling for the PTSD victims of the 'No Knock Entry' invasion.

We talked later that evening at my house and tried to put together some kind of game plan. This is bullshit, I told them. We're innocent. We haven't done anything illegal. I will never plead guilty even it means going to trial. They agreed wholeheartedly that we should fight this so they hired two criminal defense lawyers and pleaded not guilty at their indictment. As for the other ten lightbulb companies, everyone pleaded 'not guilty' and prayed that I would be found 'not guilty'.

And my scumbag partner Doug was the only 'rat' out of the twelve companies that were raided. When I reflect on that now, it's completely obvious that there was no way in hell the FBI would lose these cases. They had invested at least a year and millions of dollars on the sting operation. So the fix was in. They knew that if I was found guilty, the remaining eleven company owners would fall like dominoes.

# Chapter Ten

# HEH HEH HEH HEH HEH

My trial date finally arrived and just before I walked into the courtroom, the prosecuting lawyers, Combs and Wilson, cornered my attorneys and offered the same old three year deal. 'Kiss my ass' was my standard answer. I couldn't believe the government was still beating a dead horse with their bullshit deal. They figured the shocking reality of the courtroom would be so intimidating that I'd gratefully accept their offer and they could celebrate their victory without a trial. No white flag of surrender for me. If I had one, I'd shove it down their throats.

We all rose for the appearance of Judge Lorenzo who was reputed to be one of the toughest judges in New York. He was in his mid eighties with a head as bald and shiny as a cue ball. He shaded his small and narrow eyes with his hand as he squinted at the defense table. I thought he was sizing me up, but I quickly realized he probably couldn't see that far. His Honor dozed off several times during the week long trial as well as a couple members of the jury.

The jury consisted of eight black people and four whites. All twelve of them were casually dressed and appeared to be average working class folks. They reminded me of the types that show up in traffic court to get their speeding tickets reduced. You're there to save a hundred bucks or so, but you'll never see anyone in a suit waiting their turn because that's chump change to them. And of course, there were no 'suits' seated on the jury.

Court was called to order and the government's lead prosecuting attorney, Samuel Wilson, strolled over to the jury box teeming with confidence and began his opening statement.

"I absolutely believe that most working folks like all of you members of the jury are good citizens and make an honest living. Mr. Newman, on the other hand, does not make an honest living which is why we are here today in this court of law. Mr. Newman does not work with his hands like most of you. He is a telemarketer. His job is phoning potential customers from the comfort of his air conditioned office located on the fortieth floor of an exclusive office complex with a spectacular view of Central Park."

With the jury's full attention, Mr. Wilson continued. "He sells them products such as lightbulbs and maintenance and cleaning supplies at grossly inflated prices. He takes great pride in selling a four foot florescent lightbulb for over twenty dollars when his actual cost was only two dollars - and on and on - with every product he peddles. He entices customers into buying his products with what he calls 'gifts', but honest folks like you would call them bribes. These so called 'gifts' are usually in the form of cash.

The money is mailed discretely to the customer's home address and not his place of business where he is less likely to get caught accepting the cash bribe and being fired on the spot. When bribe money is mailed through any of the available postal delivery service companies it becomes a crime called 'mail fraud', which in addition to the other charge of 'money laundering' is why Mr. Newman sits here today. Mr. Newman's business partner of twenty years, Mr. Kaufman, is also here today because he has already pleaded guilty to these two charges."

My attorneys had prepared me for this dog and pony show, but it was not easy to maintain my poker face while Mr. Wilson manipulated the jury with outright lies and misrepresentations. "We will prove to you beyond any reasonable doubt that Mr. Newman is guilty of these crimes. He has enriched himself by breaking the law and just so the whole world is aware of his wealth, he buys himself a new Mercedes Benz every year and of course, one for his wife too."

Wilson leaned on the rail of the jury box with one hand and gestured in my direction with the other and quietly confided to the jury. "Mr. Newman sits over there at the defense table claiming his innocence and just to make sure he does not lose this trial, he is reinforced by two high priced New York lawyers who charge five hundred dollars an hour for their services. Mr. Newman is paying them a total of one thousand dollars an hour. How much do you make an hour? How many hours and days does it take you to make five hundred dollars, much less a thousand?"

Wilson concluded his award winning performance like a sanctimonious television evangelist. "Do any of you have a job where 'money laundering' and 'mail fraud' are even possible? And if you did have that opportunity to break the law to get rich, would you do it? Of course not! Thankfully most of us have a conscience, a moral compass that tells us the difference between right and wrong and guides us down the path of integrity. Evidently Mr. Newman is not equipped with such a compass."

Such is the nature of an opening statement. A lawyer can say whatever the hell he wants. Wilson's presentation was based purely on emotion. He painted an ugly picture of me with zero proof and the jury ate it up because they wanted to hang a rich guy to feel better about their own shitty jobs. He drives a Mercedes so he must be guilty, and besides, the government busted him. What more proof do you need?    Mr. Wilson had done his job exceptionally well. It appeared that the jury had already decided my guilty fate.

Then it was our turn to address the jury.

"Ladies and gentlemen," Mr. Arnett began. "Mr. Newman is here in this courtroom today because he was friends with a guy named Fred. Fred owned a small telemarketing lightbulb company that was doing well enough financially, but Fred was greedy and stupid. He wanted superstar profits so he changed the name of his company to look identical to the largest and best known wholesale company in this business. His earnings skyrocketed for a while until he was busted and indicted for fraudulent misrepresentation by imitating this powerhouse company. Pretending to be another company is clearly illegal.

He made a deal with the government and agreed to cooperate with an FBI sting operation targeting twelve companies. What did these target companies have in common? Only one thing. Fred was acquainted with the owners. That's it, ladies and gentlemen. Fred knew the owners and gave them up in exchange for a sweet government deal.

There are dozens of telemarketing lightbulb companies located throughout the United States that are still doing business today in precisely the same way that Mr. Newman's company functioned. Why are these companies still operating freely and openly and not under indictment? Because they had the good fortune not to be acquainted with Fred. The only reason Mr. Newman is sitting here today is because he knew Fred. And Fred dropped the dime on him in order to save his own skin. There are many owners of telemarketing lightbulb companies scattered across the country who must be very thankful today that they never had the misfortune of knowing Fred.

Why did the government, completely out of the blue, decide to go after the lightbulb industry? This trial is not about Mr. Newman and his alleged crimes, nor his guilt or his innocence. It is about the Federal Government. It is about their reputation, their huge investment of time, money and man hours already invested into this one year sting operation that targeted a total of twelve telemarking companies. Can you imagine the taxpayer cost for this enormously expensive production.

We are here today because the government is desperate. Their sting operation is nothing more than a witch hunt. If Mr. Newman is not found guilty, then all of the government's resources would be wasted and their reputation would take a major hit when the negative publicity exploded throughout the media. Citizens would be angry. Congress would be outraged. Taxpayers would question why the government wasted so much time and money going after a lightbulb salesman. Are you kidding me? How about going after real criminals?

Mr. Wilson works for this government and he'd like to keep his job. So instead of presenting you with hard facts to prove Mr. Newman's guilt, he is appealing to your emotions. Why? Because he has no facts. He has no hard proof. Unlike Mr. Wilson, we will present facts. We will give you indisputable proof of Mr. Newman's innocence. Please keep in mind that it is your sworn duty to base your verdict on facts and not feelings. Let me assure you that the facts will establish my client's innocence beyond any reasonable doubt."

Mr. Wilson's first witness was of course Doug Kaufman. This was the first time I had seen him since he told me that he was going to testify against me if I went to trial. The months of waiting for the court date had taken a serious toll on his health. As a rule, he generally looked like crap, but he had lost so much weight he resembled a graveyard skeleton. His shoulders were slumped and his head hung low as he nervously fidgeted in the witness chair. Typical Doug. There was no way he could look in my direction.

"How many years have you known Mr. Newman?"

Doug cleared his throat several times. "Since we were in high school."

"How many years is that?"

"About thirty, I guess."

"And how many years have you worked together, either at the same company or as partners in your own company?"

"Eighteen, nineteen years. Something like that."

"Were you aware that some of your business practices were possibly illegal?"

"Well there were some things I didn't feel comfortable with and every time I tried to talk with Scott about it, he always said not to worry because we are not doing anything illegal. So I trusted him."

"You trusted Mr. Newman's judgement?"

"Yes, why wouldn't I. We've been friends and partners for years."

"Were you familiar with a crime known as 'Trade Based Money Laundering'?"

"Not at the time, no."

"But you had doubts regarding some of your company's business practices?"

"Yes, but like I said, I trusted Scott that everything was Okay."

"Did your company invoice the buyers at prices well above 'free market value' which resulted in a large increase in profit for you, the seller?"

"Yes, we did."

"When you used the profit you gained from overpriced invoices, were you aware that the profit automatically became 'dirty' money and that you cleaned it by using it to sell more products to other customers?"

"Not really. I believed that Scott would never get me involved in something like that."

"But he did involve you whether you were aware of the law or not."

"I guess so."

"So you did the right thing and pleaded guilty to money laundering."

"Objection, 'leading the witness'," Arnett contended.

"Sustained," barked the judge just as he was nodding off again.

"Do you think Mr. Newman was aware of the law?"

"Objection, that calls for 'speculation'," Arnett declared.

"Sustained."

"Mr. Newman has referred to himself as the 'King of Benjamins'. Where does that term come from?"

Doug exhaled slowly. "It's a name he gave himself. He put fake hundred dollar bills in Priority Overnight envelopes and told buyers that the real money was on the way."

"So this was Mr. Newman's strategy for bribing customers?"

"Objection, Your Honor," Arnett said with intensity.

"Mr. Wilson, I'm cautioning you…"

"I withdraw the question, Your Honor. At this time, I would like to offer into evidence for the prosecution, 'Exhibit A'."

From the ceiling, a large video screen slowly descended. 'Exhibit A' was an image of a fake one hundred dollar bill.

"Do you recognize this image, Mr. Kaufman?"

"Yes, I do."

"Do you know what this image represents?"

"Yes, it's Scott Newman's marketing card."

"And Mr. Newman would send these cards to buyers?"

"Yes."

"For what purpose?"

"It was a 'sales incentive' to buy products."

"Would you please read the bold phrase in capital letters."

"The real money is on the way."

"The real money is on the way. That is certainly one heck of a 'sales incentive'. Isn't this just an outright 'bribe'?"

"Objection!"

"Sustained. The jury will disregard that statement. Mr. Wilson, do you have any further questions before we take a recess?"

"Just a couple more Your Honor."

Wilson turned back to Doug. "Did you observe Mr. Newman sending cash to customers as 'gifts'?"

"Yes."

"And were you aware of the cash value of those 'gifts'?"

"It varied from a few hundred to several thousand dollars, depending on the buyer."

"And how were these cash 'gifts' received by the customer?"

"The money was placed in an Overnight or Two Day delivery envelope."

"No further questions, your honor," Wilson said politely.

Doug was visibly shaken. The judge was pissed off because his nap had been interrupted and called for a short recess. Doug slinked off the stand like a whipped dog. When court resumed and Doug returned to the witness stand, I thought he was going to pass out while he waited for my attorney to begin his cross examination. Mr. Arnett prolonged his leisurely stroll to the witness stand which only added to Doug's misery as he squirmed with dread.

"Mr. Kaufman, you've pleaded guilty to the charges of money laundering and mail fraud, is that correct?"

Beads of sweat formed on Doug's brow as he stammered, "Yes, I did."

"Would you please define 'money laundering' as you understand it for the jury."

"Well, Mr. Wilson already did that."

"We would like to hear your definition, Mr. Kaufman, specifically how it relates to your guilty plea. In other words, describe the crime you confessed to."

Doug sucked in as much air as he could muster. "Okay, we sold products at inflated prices and used the profits to purchase more products and then we continued to sell other companies."

"To the best of your knowledge, was the profit you made from selling products actually 'dirty' money?"

"Yes…no…I don't know. It's really complicated."

"No Mr. Kaufman, it's not complicated. What you just described is not a crime, it's called capitalism. It's how we do business in this country. As a business owner yourself, isn't your goal to make money? And if you don't make money, the business fails. Isn't that how it works?"

Doug shrugged his shoulders.

"Did you and your wife recently go on an 'all expenses paid' one week vacation to Florida?"

"Yes we did."

"Did you pay for the trip?"

"No."

"If you didn't pay for this Florida vacation then who did?"

"It was a 'gift' from Universal Supply, the company I purchase most of our merchandise from."

"A 'gift', Mr. Kaufman?"

"Well yes, it was a 'gift' to show their appreciation for my business."

"Did you ever suspect that this was a company attempt to bribe you?"

"Objection," Wilson said evenly.

"Have you ever offered 'gifts' to your customers to show your appreciation for their business?"

"Of course, everyone does it."

"Everyone does it? Would you say that 'gifts' are simply a common way of doing business?"

"Yes."

"Could you describe for the jury the types of 'gifts' you offered your customers."

"Paid up Visa cards. MasterCard vouchers. Things like that."

"And what was the cash value of these 'gifts'?"

"One hundred to two hundred dollars. Sometimes up to five hundred dollars."

"Did you ever offer a 'gift' of cash?"

"No, I just sent out cards."

"What is the difference between cash and a card that represents cash?"

"Well, cash is cash, it looks like a bribe."

"And a Visa card with a cash value is not a bribe?"

"It's not the same thing," Doug stammered out of frustration.

"Because cash looks like a bribe?" Arnett summarized.

Doug didn't respond. He just shrugged his shoulders again.

"How many cards did you normally send out as a typical 'gift'?"

"About two or three."

"Did you ever send more than two or three gift cards to a single customer?"

"Well yes."

"How many cards would you send to your best customers?"

"Fifteen to twenty or so."

"Twenty or so. Let's do the math, Mr. Kaufman. If each card had a cash value of one to two hundred dollars, then we're looking at a 'gift' of two to four thousand dollars."

Arnett waited while Doug squirmed in his chair. "Did you call yourself the 'King of Visa Cards'?"

"Objection," Wilson complained.

"Sustained. The jury will disregard that last statement. Please limit yourself to relevant questions Mr. Arnett."

"Yes, Your Honor."

Arnett approached Doug again. "What was the cash value of your one week Florida vacation last month?"

"I don't really know."

"Based on your first class flight, your five star hotel, your meals and so forth, would you estimate that the cost of your holiday was roughly five thousand dollars?"

Doug shifted in his chair and shrugged.

"So this Florida holiday, the 'gift' that you accepted, had a cash value of about five thousand dollars, would you agree, Mr. Kaufman?"

"I guess so."

"Could you please explain the difference between a Florida vacation package valued at five thousand dollars and a stack of Visa cards valued at five thousand dollars and five thousand dollars in cash."

"Objection," Wilson stated in a monotone which diminished the impact Arnett intended to have on the jury.

"My apologies, Your Honor."

"If I have correctly understood your definition of a 'bribe', Mr. Kaufman, a cash 'gift' consisting of a few one hundred dollar bills is actually a 'bribe' while the 'gift' of a Florida vacation is simply an expression of appreciation."

"Objection," Wilson repeated in a monotone.

Fully awake, the Judge cautioned Arnett again.

Arnett nodded his head apologetically to the Judge, shifted gears and continued with a different line of questioning.

"Did you or Mr. Newman ever mislead any buyers by quoting them a lower price and then billing or invoicing them at a higher price?"

"No sir, we did not."

"Were you aware that companies can legally charge any price they want as long as they are not misquoting or misleading the buyer?"

"Yes, of course."

"When a buyer declined to buy your product because the price was too high, did you ever attempt to negotiate a lower price in order to make the sale?"

"Yes."

"Why would you lower the price?"

"So we wouldn't lose the sale."

"To the best of your knowledge, did you or Mr. Newman ever attempt to force or coerce a buyer to purchase your product?"

"No never."

"To the best of your knowledge, did you or Mr. Newman ever send a product to a buyer even though they did not want the product?"

"No."

"Are you aware, Mr. Kaufman, of the twelve owners charged with 'mail fraud', Mr. Newman is the only one facing the additional charge of 'money laundering'?"

Mr. Wilson instantly expressed his objection and before the judge could respond, Mr. Arnett quickly withdrew the question and began another line of inquiry.

"You testified that you always spoke with Mr. Newman about certain business practices that made you uncomfortable and he would tell you not to worry because you weren't doing anything illegal. Is that correct?"

"Yes."

"Did you seek an outside point of view to confirm the legality of your concerns?"

"Yes, I would call my attorney."

"And did your attorney confirm the legality of your business practices?"

"Yes, he did."

"Did he ever caution you that any of your practices were illegal or potentially illegal?"

"No, not really."

"So every time you consulted with your lawyer, he verified Mr. Newman's position that you were not doing anything illegal?"

Doug turned another shade of white and squeaked out a 'yes' while Mr. Arnett tersely concluded. "It seems to me that you pleaded guilty not only to a crime that you cannot define, but you also do not even understand. Why would anyone do that unless they were threatened with - let's say - ten years in prison."

"Objection, Your Honor," Wilson leaped out of his chair. "Badgering the witness."

"Sustained. Do you have a question for the witness Mr. Arnett?"

"Did you make a deal with the government in exchange for your guilty plea?"

Sweat rolled slowly down the deep lines of Doug's haggard face.

"Yes".

"What were the details of that deal?"

"No jail time and surrendering my savings and investments."

"And how much did that amount to?"

Doug mumbled his answer.

"I'm sorry, Mr. Kaufman, would you mind speaking up so the jury can hear you."

"Around two million dollars."

"Around two million dollars," he repeated and paused a moment for the jury to absorb that incredible amount of money. "Did all that money come from your employment in the lightbulb business?"

"Oh no," Doug suddenly perked up. "I've been saving since I was a teenager."

"How many years have you been saving then?"

"Over thirty years."

"How much of that money would you say has been laundered?"

"Objection," Mr. Wilson fumed.

"Sustained," confirmed the Judge.

"So Mr. Kaufman, let's be clear. During the past thirty years, you have saved over two million dollars, a lot of which did not come from your work in the lightbulb industry and yet you gave ALL of the two million dollars to the government as part of your deal?"

"Yes."

"Did you agree to testify against Mr. Newman as part of your deal with the government?"

"Yes," Doug moaned softly and hung his head even lower.

"You've been friends and partners for over twenty years and yet here you are, sitting in this courtroom testifying under oath to save yourself and throw Mr. Newman under the bus."

"Objection," Wilson screamed.

"Sustained. The jury will disregard that statement. You're treading a fine line, Mr. Arnett," the Judge cautioned.

"I apologize, Your Honor. At this time, I would like to enter into evidence, 'Exhibit B' for the defense."

The video screen rolled down from the ceiling revealing the image of a 'paid up' Gift Card with the cash value of five hundred dollars prominently featured in two corners of the card.

"Mr. Kaufman, you stated earlier that you routinely sent 'paid up' cards to your customers as 'gifts'. Is the card on the screen an accurate example?"

"Yes, it is."

"Would you please explain to the jury how this card functions."

"Well, this card has a value of five hundred dollars."

"So the receiver of this 'gift' card can go into any store or restaurant and buy goods or services or meals by presenting the card as payment."

"Yes"

"And it would be accepted for payment, the same as cash?"

"Yes."

"In other words, it functions the same way as cash?"

"It has cash value, but technically it's not cash. It's a card," Doug emphasized.

"Do you purchase these cards with cash?"

"Yes, but it's still not the same thing," Doug protested.

"Then what is the difference, Mr. Kaufman? I'm sure the jury would like to know."

"Cash can be seen as a bribe, but a Visa card is just a 'gift' card."

Arnett clicks his remote and Mr. Newman's marketing card appears on the screen with the Gift Card.

"Which of these two cards represents a specific cash value?"

"Objection, Your Honor. Irrelevant."

"Overruled. Let's see where Mr. Arnett is going with this line of questioning. The witness may answer the question."

"Okay, the Gift Card."

"What is the cash value of the Gift Card?"

"Five hundred dollars."

"Is there a cash value displayed on Mr. Newman's card?"

"No, but it says that 'the real money is on the way'."

"The 'real money is on the way'. Is that a 'sales incentive' or a guarantee?"

"Objection. Leading the witness."

"Sustained."

"In your earlier testimony, you referred to Mr. Newman's marketing card as a 'sales incentive'. Is that correct?"

"Yes."

"Would you agree that a Gift Card is also a 'sales incentive'?"

"Objection."

Arnett moves toward the video screen and pauses next to it. He faces the jury and points to the cards. "Which of these cards would be accepted by a merchant for payment of a product or service?"

"Objection."

"Sustained."

"What were the average values of the Visa cards you sent out as 'gifts'?"

"Between two and five hundred dollars each."

"Did you pay cash for those Visa cards?"

"Yes."

"How many cards, on average, did you send out to your customers?"

"It depended on the customer. Sometimes I'd send a couple cards worth two hundred dollars each and other times, if it was a real good customer, I'd send out eight to ten cards with a value of five hundred dollars each."

"Ok, Mr. Kaufman, let's do the math one more time. Two Visa cards valued at two hundred dollars each equals four hundred dollars. Eight to ten cards worth five hundred dollars a piece adds up to four or five thousand dollars. Please explain again, the difference between five thousand dollars in cash and the five thousand dollars in cash that you paid for the Visa cards."

"Objection."

"No further questions, Your Honor."

I wanted to high five my attorney when he returned to our table but I resisted the impulse. It probably wouldn't look too good in front of the jury. It was hard to tell what they were thinking, but at least a small seed of uncertainty was planted in their minds.

We began my defense by calling our bookkeeper to the stand who confirmed that we paid taxes on every dime we made. She was followed by an IRS agent who had fully audited our books and verified our bookkeeper's testimony and stated that our books and tax returns were clean and he found no evidence to indicate we were hiding money.

Mr. Wilson sat comfortably in his chair and in full view of the jury, shrugged his shoulders, a gesture that clearly indicated 'so what if he paid his taxes'.

From his table where he remained seated, Mr. Wilson addressed the IRS Agent. "I only have one question for you sir. Is it possible for Mr. Newman to hide money from the IRS?

"Yes it is, but not in this particular case."

"Thank you. No further questions," Wilson casually concluded, satisfied with the cloud of doubt he created on the faces of the jury.

Our next witness was Bert Langer, an ex FBI agent who worked as an expert witness in money laundering trials and in my case, his testimony would represent my innocence. Mr. Arnett reviewed Mr. Langer's background and qualifications for the jury and began the questioning by asking when money laundering officially became a crime in the United States.

"It was during the 1920's," Mr. Langer began, "when Al Capone was running bootleg liquor during the alcohol prohibition era of our country's history. Capone owned a string of laundromats where he would launder or clean his 'dirty' money from his liquor bootlegging and other illegal operations. Thus the term 'money laundering'. Because his laundromats were making huge profits, it drew the unwanted attention of the US Treasury

Department and Capone was eventually convicted of tax evasion, but never 'money laundering' even though it was obvious."

"In your opinion is Mr. Newman guilty of money laundering?"

"No sir, selling lightbulbs is not quite the same as liquor running or drug dealing."

"The prosecution has defined money laundering as 'the process of making illegally gained proceeds or 'dirty' money - appear clean or legal". In your opinion, does selling lightbulbs represent 'dirty' money?"

"Absolutely not."

Mr. Wilson leaned forward and addressed Mr. Langer from his chair. "Are you being paid by Mr. Newman's defense team to testify here today?"

"Yes I am."

"Thank you. No further questions."

Wilson's strategy to simply dismiss our witness as a compensated member of my defense team intensified the doubt that was growing in the minds of the jury.

We called three different character witnesses to testify on my behalf and Mr. Wilson proceeded to shoot down all three of them concluding that even though they believed that I was a nice guy, they were not familiar with the details of my business operation. Therefore, their testimony was irrelevant. Only my partner, Doug Kaufman, knew what was really going on and he pleaded guilty.

There were no more witnesses to call for my defense and after five grueling days, Mr. Wilson began his closing argument by lowering the huge video screen in front of the jury. The lights were dimmed and one of my bonus checks was enlarged to fill up the entire screen. The amount was thirty thousand dollars.

"That's just one of Mr. Newman's bonus checks that he receives throughout the year. Isn't that about how much most of you make in one full year of hard work?"

Every member of the jury stared grimly at the screen trying to wrap their minds around the obscene size of that single check.

"And it's not the only check Mr. Newman received."

Wilson deliberately paused for the dramatic effect he knew the second check would produce. It was also for thirty thousand dollars. Soft gasps filled the sudden stillness of the courtroom.

With each click of the remote control, Wilson slammed another emotional nail into my trial coffin. There were a total of six checks ranging between twenty five and thirty thousand dollars each. When all the checks were on full display, Mr. Wilson quietly addressed the stunned jury members.

"Mr. Newman received those six checks one week at a time between Thanksgiving and Christmas. I'm sure he had a very Merry Christmas. How about you?"

Wilson folded his arms and faced the jury again. "His lifelong friend and partner in crime already confessed. What more proof do you need?"

Amy leaned over the railing and touched my shoulder. "Look at their faces, Scott. We are totally screwed."

Amy was right. The jury maintained a collective glare of utter disgust. Most of them made no attempt to disguise their feelings of contempt for me. Here was their big chance to take down a rich guy even though those checks were perfectly legal.

My attorney approached the jury and placed his hands on the barrister and began his closing argument.

"Let's say that a friend or a loved one of yours has a serious accident. You call 911 for an ambulance or you jump in your car and race to the nearest emergency room. When you arrive, do you ask about the prices of health care or do you expect immediate medical attention? As you pace up and down in the waiting room are you thinking about the financial cost of the accident or are you praying that everything will be okay?

Fortunately, most of the time everything works out, your loved one is going to be fine. You are grateful and relieved. You can breathe normally again...until you get the bill. You can't believe your eyes. You are shocked and outraged by the astronomical charges. Normal items like bandaids and bandages are insanely overpriced. The bill runs into thousands of dollars. And your first clear thought is that your insurance better cover this. But what happens when your insurance doesn't cover the costs? At that moment, you become responsible for the unpaid balance. What happens if you don't have insurance in the first place? Bad news gets worse. You are responsible for the entire bill.

Let me give you an example of an outrageous medical bill. A Florida hospital charged a patient $193,000 to treat pneumonia. His insurance covered $9,600 leaving him a debt of $183,400. He had no choice but to declare bankruptcy. Ridiculous medical bills are forcing more and more Americans into bankruptcy every day. Most of you are just an accident away from the same fate."

Mr. Arnett was on a roll. "There was an article recently published in a major magazine that investigated grossly inflated hospital charges. They discovered that one hospital in New Jersey was charging $143.24 for syringe needles that cost them only eighty cents each. That is a markup of over one thousand per cent. Where is the FBI investigation in this outrageous situation? They also discovered an ambulance company that was taking kickbacks from a hospital for delivering auto accident victims to their emergency room even though other hospitals were much closer. Isn't there a moral obligation to provide immediate first aid rather than delaying medical attention and gambling with the patient's health.

These examples of blatant overpricing and kickbacks come at the risk of your health and in some cases your life. So here's a head scratching question. Why is it okay for the health care industry to mark up prices and not the lightbulb industry? Why isn't the FBI looking into these obvious double standards? Why is Mr. Newman sitting here for marking up prices on lightbulbs? Are any of you risking bankruptcy or your health for purchasing lightbulbs from Mr. Newman?"

Arnett paused for a moment and addressed the jury again. "Let's take a look at the facts of the trial, something the prosecuting attorneys have conveniently managed to avoid. Of the twelve owners charged by the government with 'mail fraud', only Mr. Newman is charged with 'money laundering'.

Since all twelve companies conduct their business operations in a similar fashion, the question I have for you is simple. Why has Mr. Newman been singled out? And the answer is quite obvious. In exchange for a government plea bargain deal, his business partner of twenty years pleaded guilty to a crime he did not even know he committed and was completely unable to give a coherent definition of that crime.

Mr. Kaufman, however, was able to define the difference between a gift and a 'bribe'. According to Mr. Kaufman, a 'bribe' consists of hard cash, for example, a one hundred dollar bill, while a one hundred dollar Visa card, paid for with cash by Mr. Kaufman is only a 'gift'. A 'gift' like his Florida vacation. The list of 'gifts' goes on and on: season tickets to Dallas Cowboy games or any other professional sporting event, dinners at five star restaurants, product 'samples' such as clothing, cosmetics, furniture, maybe even a new car. These 'gifts' are offered, of course, as a sincere expression of appreciation for conducting business. And every major company in America and the rest of the world functions in the same way.

222

What's the difference between the 'King of Benjamins' and the 'King of Visa cards'? Which brings us back to the central question of this case: why is Mr. Newman being singled out?

Mr. Kaufman has testified against Mr. Newman as a government witness. How reliable is a witness who received a deal from the government? How reliable is a witness who confessed to a crime he cannot describe? How reliable is a witness who was threatened with ten years in prison and surrendered two million dollars to the government? Mr. Kaufman is simply a pawn of this government. They need a conviction to justify the time and money they have wasted on what is nothing more than a witch hunt.

Let's review the facts of this case again. The company bookkeeper confirmed that all taxes were paid. An IRS Agent fully audited the books and verified the tax returns were clean and he found no evidence that profits were being hidden. A former FBI Agent who specialized in money laundering schemes testified that he found absolutely no evidence of such a crime. And Mr. Kaufman's private attorney assured him on several occasions that both he and Mr. Newman were doing nothing illegal.

This trial is a textbook case of the government railroading an innocent man to prison with no solid proof in order to justify their failed 'sting' operation. Mr. Newman conducted his business in exactly the same way that all telemarketing lightbulb companies operate. Again, I ask you, as members of this jury, why is Mr. Newman being singled out?"

I scanned the skeptical faces of the jury and I don't think they listened to a single word my lawyer said. He stressed that justice is served by considering the facts of the case, and not to be distracted by the lies and manipulations of the prosecution. Taxes were paid on the bonus checks. It was standard accounting practice to pay all taxes before the end of the year. Unlike Al Capone, I paid my taxes. They could not convict me of crimes the government failed to prove I committed.

Or could they?

Court was adjourned and the jury convened for the verdict.

The jury deliberated for less than three hours so I knew I was screwed. As the jurors made their way back to their seats, most of them concentrated on the floor while some of them just stared me down and made no attempt to hide their vindictive feelings. 'Victory! We nailed a rich guy!' My lawyer, Mr. Arnett, placed his hand on my shoulder which I took as an empty gesture of comfort. In reality, I could feel the knife slowly sinking into my back.

My lawyers were much too cozy with the government District Attorneys and after the guilty verdict was delivered, they packed their leather briefcases, shook hands like old buddies and exchanged pleasantries no doubt confirming arrangements to meet for drinks later that evening. Am I suggesting there was a conspiracy? Did my lawyers already knew the fix was in before I retained them?

Maybe.

Maybe not.

But looking back now, I can see clearly that there was no way in hell the government would lose this case.

Amy had a blank look on her face. Although she had anticipated the guilty verdict, it did not prepare her for the reality that stung like an Iron Mike Tyson left hook.

Leon and Marsha were crushed. They were in the courtroom every day and were absolutely certain of my innocence and theirs as well. Now they faced a similar outcome at their trial which was coming up in a month. They mortgaged their two properties and drained their savings accounts to pay their expensive defense lawyers who assured them that their case was totally different from mine. They were not charged with money laundering so there was no way they could lose.

However, two weeks before the trial, Leon and Marsha had already shelled out over three hundred thousand dollars in fees. When they confided their dire financial situation to their lawyers, suddenly all confidence disappeared in defending their case. Leon and Marsha were advised to plead guilty and if they refused, the lawyers would not be able to represent them at trial. The double-dealing lawyers also assured them that if they entered a guilty plea, Leon would only have to do three years in prison and Marsha would not have any jail time at all. Of course, the judge saw things a little differently and sentenced Leon to three years and Marsha served a year and a day.

The government strategy of convicting me at trial created the domino effect they planned from the beginning. Every indicted owner of the ten remaining lightbulb companies pleaded guilty to the single charge of mail fraud and waived the right to a trial and were sentenced to three years in prison.

Thanks to Doug, I was the only one charged and convicted for money laundering. His guilty plea and testimony against me cost an additional three years in prison for a total of six years behind bars. Ironically, Doug's naive belief that the government would honor his 'deal' didn't quite pan out. He had already surrendered his two million dollars in retirement savings in exchange for the promise of no jail time.

I wish I could have been a fly on the wall of the courtroom when Doug stood before the sentencing judge brimming with confidence and relief that his ordeal was finally over. The judge shuffled through some paperwork and somberly declared that he had carefully considered the government's recommendation for no jail time, however, the nature of the crimes required not only compensation for the victims, but also an obligatory debt to society that must be paid. He sentenced Doug to three years in a federal penitentiary. The gavel slammed down with a conclusive bang. The cold metal of handcuffs snapped around Doug's wrists and for the first time in his life, he had nowhere to run or hide.

Instead of walking through the double courtroom doors of freedom to exhale his long awaited sigh of relief, Doug was unceremoniously escorted out the back to a nondescript white van that delivered him to his new permanent residence surrounded with barbed wire fences and ominous guard towers. I think most people are aware of what happens to rats and child molesters in prison.

While the convicted owners were serving time in prison it was business as usual for the rest of lightbulb companies that were not raided. In fact, most of the jailed owners re-opened new telemarketing lightbulb businesses after they were released and continued to operate in precisely the same manner that sent them to prison in the first place. There were no lessons learned here. The industry was not 'cleaned up'. New regulations or laws were not enacted. Absolutely nothing changed. The only result of the sting operation was that the FBI and the government had a nice new feather in its cap they could brag about on the TV talk show circuit and that was that.

I was forbidden by the sentencing judge to work in the lightbulb industry after serving the six year sentence he handed down and he warned me (there was no written agreement!) that if I violated the ban from the industry, I would be going back to prison for a much longer time. I assured the judge that would never happen because I had learned from my mistakes and was looking forward to starting over with a clean slate. So I served my time uneventfully except for one tiny detail - I was still making piles of money from the three companies I co-owned with Buddy. You gotta love burner cell phones!

After my release from prison, Amy and I settled in a modest condo on the big island of Hawaii overlooking the vast, aqua blue Pacific Ocean. (Thanks for the idea, Fred. I actually believed your bullshit retirement story of living here. Too bad you turned rat and the government took every last penny you and Rhonda had.) Every day we would take long walks on the beach and just relax in our lounge chairs and let our minds drift with the peaceful rhythm of the ocean waves lapping at our feet.

Even though I no longer had a need for a cell phone, I still received an occasional call from Buddy.

"How's the weather over there?"

"Beautiful as usual. My toes are covered in warm sand instead of frost bite from shoveling tons of snow."

"Are you sitting down?"

"More or less. I'm just chilling out in my lounge chair and watching the usual parade of bikinis strolling by. What's up?"

"We just had a spectacular record breaking month, partner. Profits were up by over thirty per cent and your bonus check shredded any pay day you ever had before."

I raised my tropical drink. "Cheers partner," and whooped out my Woody Woodpecker money making victory yell:


HEH HEH HEH HEH HEH

HEH HEH HEH HEH HEH

HEH HEH HEH HEH HEH HEH HEH

Th-th-th-that's all folks!!

Made in the USA
Middletown, DE
31 August 2019